THE HAUNTED MOOR

David Mcillorum

Printed in Great Britain by Amazon
ISBN:978-1520339825

For my wife Sue

FOREWORD

Have you seen a ghost? Millions worldwide claim to have, but can they reach out from beyond the grave itself and influence the living?

I remember a story my mother told me over 40 years ago, when I was growing up with my younger brothers and sisters in a small village in Cornwall.

It was the height of summer and a family across the road were in the front garden enjoying the sunshine when their little boy came screeching out of the house. After calming the child, they learned he had been in the living room and poking around behind the live television set with a knitting needle in his hand. The boy claimed he had been pulled back to safety by a pair of old hands that clutched his shoulders.

'Old hands...old hands,' he kept saying.

I have no doubt in the sincerity of a child...but I'll let you decide...

David Mcillorum

PROLOGUE

The van slowed as it approached the bend in the track. The driver knew the area like the back of his hand, having taken this route umpteen times in the past, but tonight he struggled to recognise the spot he was searching for and had visited only hours before in the daylight. Everything looked different in the dark, especially out here in the middle of nowhere. There were no street lamps, no buildings or familiar man made shapes to help him, not even a single telegraph pole, nothing except miles upon miles of barren landscape.

He was relieved when the headlights revealed the dirt track snaking away from the main trail and he brought the van to an abrupt halt, his heart beating faster as the adrenaline kicked in and the gravity of what he was about to do loomed ever greater in his mind.

For a few seconds, he sat there with his hands clutching the steering wheel and he took a couple of deep breaths, not to calm himself, but to suppress the dull ache in his forehead that was threatening to turn into a fully blown headache. He didn't need that, not now.

He went around the back and pulled open

the van doors. The knotted end of the sack was visible as it lay there in the moonlight and for a moment, he glanced around to check no one was watching then admonished himself for forgetting where he was. There wasn't another soul for miles. Leaning in he dragged the sack out, dipped his knees and slung it awkwardly over his shoulder before taking the shovel that had been lying alongside it.

By the light of the full moon, like something only witnessed in some grisly horror film, he took the narrow dirt track across the moor until he found the grave he'd prepared earlier that day. The sack was dumped in without a care in the world and he started shovelling in dirt from the pile right next to him.

He felt no regret and nothing weighed heavy on his mind. Bitch! he thought, as he walked back to the van.

ONE

Maddie bounded down the stairs, her short pony tail bobbing behind with each step she took. Skilfully, she managed to read the mobile phone in her hand whilst avoiding the backpack leaning against the wall in the narrow hallway. The smell of cooked bacon became more intense as she entered the small kitchen, her sharp blue eyes glued to the phone.

Her mum was cooking breakfast. 'Good timing Maddie,' she said, keeping her eyes on the frying pan. 'You want one, or two eggs?'

Maddie sat on the end of the breakfast bench, then shuffled across to the middle. 'One will be fine mum thanks,' she replied, fingers deftly texting a message on the tiny keys, whilst her free hand grabbed the mug on the table and brought it to her lips. She took two sips of the steaming coffee and set it back down. Holding the phone with both hands, elbows on the table, she checked the message she was about to send.

'Hi Jodie. Catching the 9.21 from Plymouth. Due to get into St Austell for 10.22. Will text you if there's going to be a delay, otherwise see you later in sunny Cornwall.'

'Sunny Cornwall,' wasn't a presumption on her part or a light-hearted joke. It was the middle of summer, Plymouth and most of the South West of England enjoying some unusually fine and prolonged weather for a change. In defiance of the doom merchant's warnings that climate change was disrupting the natural rhythm of the seasons and nothing would ever be the same again. But there had been little evidence of that, Maddie had thought, when she'd opened the bedroom curtains earlier to another bright sunny morning. Her thumb hit the send button and the phone bleeped instantly telling her the message had been sent.

'That Jodie?' The attractive thirty-nine-year-old placed a plate of food in front of her daughter and another one on her side. 'She okay?' She slid onto the bench opposite Maddie, flicking a single strand of blonde hair away from her eyes.

Maddie pushed the phone aside. 'Jodie's fine. I was just letting her know what time to meet me at the station.'

Picking up her knife and fork she tucked into her breakfast of bacon, eggs, fried bread and beans. She would need a good meal this morning, where she was going.

Her mum took a sip of tea; she preferred it to coffee. 'Don't worry kidda, I'll get you to the station on time,' she joked, glancing at the kitchen clock on the wall behind Maddie. 'You've got plenty of time yet. Another hour, and then we'll shoot off.'

'That's okay. Everything's packed anyway and I don't think I've forgotten anything.'

'Toothbrush?'

'Yep, got it.'

'Taking your camera?'

'Nope. One on the phones good enough to be honest.'

'Spare underwear?'

'Of course,' Maddie said, giving her a quirky look across the table.

'Alright, just checking that's all. I'll shut up now, shall I?' she laughed, recalling how she'd been at that age too, how she'd felt all grown up and independent at the ripe old age of nineteen and how irrelevant advice had seemed from anyone over thirty. And especially if it came from her parents. Anyway, thirty was over the hill. It was positively ancient! If you were over fifty – the dreaded grey hair brigade – well, that was it; you'd had your fair share of living and were one foot in

3

the grave already. What could they possibly know anyway? They had their own little world to look back on, to reminisce over, whilst she had everything to look forward to and the world was her oyster. It was like chalk and cheese.

Looking across at her daughter now, she saw an older version of the little girl she once was: the same Maddie with the pert little nose, the mousey blonde hair, and the sharp sparkling blue eyes. It was only the full breasts and curvy figure that made her different now: a woman. No longer a minor in the eyes of the law and responsible for her actions but still a teenager all the same, and not yet turned twenty. Hopefully, in a few years after she'd gained her degree and carved herself a career, she might find a nice man, settle down not too far away and make her a proud grandmother. She knew she had to allow Maddie the space and independence her own parents hadn't allowed her, or risk alienating and pushing her daughter away altogether. So, when Maddie had told her she was thinking about going hiking in Cornwall with Jodie for a few days during the university summer holiday, she had gone along with the idea, albeit reluctantly.

'It's only for three days,' Maddie had reassured her. 'And the weathers perfect too. A couple of nights in a tent will be a doddle.'

'But you've never done anything like that

before. You don't mind sharing a tent with a few creepy crawlies then?' The light-hearted question was not an attempt to put her daughter off.

'Ha, unless you class Jodie as a bug,' she grinned. 'It won't be as bad as all that. It's not like it's the middle of the jungle or anything, is it? And anyway, Jodie showed me the route on the internet. Everything about the trail is on there if you want to have a look.'

'The internet?' The revelation shouldn't have surprised her. Maddie was always telling her if you wanted to find anything out you only had to look on the web.

'Just do a search on Bodmin Moor Copper Trail. There's a whole heap of stuff on there.'

Which is exactly what she did, most of her fears soon disappearing when she saw the intended hike was around the edge of Bodmin Moor (not across the moor itself) on an established walking route. Not some ramble across open country with just a map and a compass and no one for company except the local wildlife. On the first day, they would start at Minions village and walk the eight miles to St Neot. Day two would be a thirteen-mile hike to Bodmin, followed by a ten miler to St Breward on the last day. The full Copper trail was a sixty-mile circular route, taking in many of the moors most striking features of Neolithic monuments, ancient stone circles and tiny secluded hamlets. It was one of Cornwall's true remaining wilderness areas, eighty square miles of moorland dotted with tors, 18th century disused mine workings and huge granite outcrops. The pair were only going to do half that distance. Still, it was only natural to worry. It was a mother's prerogative.

She guessed being a single parent had made her more protective towards Maddie. The only time she'd spent away from home being the occasional sleep over at a friend's house during her early teen years. When she had gained a place at Plymouth University, she had continued living at home, which made financial sense as the university was only a bus ride away and meant she didn't have to pay for meals or accommodation. Maddie's grandparents had been a great help over the years. Like most grandparents, they doted on her, insisting they would pay towards her university fees provided she secured a place. There was no way she could have funded her daughter's education from her thirty hours a week job without a working father around to help with the costs.

She'd been carrying Maddie for six months, when Tom had been killed in a car crash on the A30, a lorry skidding across the road in front of him. The pile up had claimed the lives of two others that evening, two more grief stricken families left to pick up the pieces. The inquest said he had died instantly; June 13th 1997, a date firmly etched in her mind. The Police report said the lorry driver had been using his mobile when the accident happened. He got ten years in prison, but served only half of that after remission. A complete joke, she had thought at the time, the judge constrained by the sentencing guidelines that laid out the maximum punishment available for certain crimes. It hadn't been a premeditated act of murder, which would have resulted in a much stiffer sentence and probably life. What angered her more than anything was that Tom's death was completely avoidable. Ironically, her husband's killer, and that's what she thought of him; a *killer*, could be living in the same town as them or even in the same street. He could have been waiting in the checkout queue behind her when she did the weekly shop; she could even have served *him*, smiling at him and making polite conversation like she did with every other customer.

'You okay mum?' Maddie asked, noticing the reflective look. 'Penny for them?' She had finished her breakfast; baked bean juice the only remnants left on her plate.

'Oh – away with the fairies, that's all,' she said dismissively, getting up from her seat and taking her empty plate to the sink. She came back for Maddie's. 'Finished?'

'Uh-uh.' Maddie was back on her phone and

checking her emails. There were two: one telling her she could claim back Payment Protection Insurance if she had a credit card or a bank loan, the other saying: 'CONGRATULATIONS YOU'VE WON A PRIZE', in a competition she hadn't even entered and to text back so she could claim it. Yes, Maddie thought, the prize being a five-pound charge to her phone if she was stupid enough to reply to what was an obvious scam. It was as bad as the other one doing the rounds. A few of the university students had almost been caught out by the phone call telling them their computer was infected with a virus which was spreading further over the web every time they connected to the internet. Of course, the caller could fix it if you gave them remote access to your computer and they would get rid of the virus, except the only thing the con artists would get rid of was the balance in your bank account, not to mention theft of your personal details that could later be used in some sort of identity fraud. Maddie was grateful for the weekly student newsletter that had saved many of them from the latest information technology fraud's that seemed to be on the increase.

She opened the weather app on her phone. Today was Friday. The forecast for the weekend and into next week was sunny, with a zero percent chance of rain. Before opening her 'sticky notes' phone application (she wondered how anyone had ever managed without a smartphone years ago) she drank the last of her coffee, then read through the checklist she had been given over a week ago, ticking each item off in her head: sleeping bag, foam bedroll, torch, spare batteries, toiletries, socks, underwear...by the time she had got through it all, wondering how she had ever managed to squeeze it all into the medium sized backpack sitting in the hall. But she had and Jodie had been right all along, the ex-Girl Guide having sent her a list of everything she would need for the trip. The only item missing from the list was a two-man tent (two-woman tent in their case) which Jodie said she would bring. The domed tent weighed less than two pounds, had a built-in mosquito net – they wouldn't need that, would they? – and came with its own sewn in ground sheet, popular apparently with festival goers. At least there was no mud where she was going and welly boots wouldn't be needed, she thought with amusement.

'Sure you've got everything? Have you charged your phone?' Mum had finished washing up and was drying her hands on the tea towel.

Maddie pushed herself up from the table. 'Yep, everything ticks off.' She joined her at the sink. 'I don't mind drying. And yes, the phones charged,' she added, taking the tea towel in her hands and picking up a plate from the drainer. 'I hope I can get a signal out there,' she said, wondering if the same thought had occurred to Jodie.

Mum frowned. 'Around the moor? Yes – I would think so Maddie. They've got masts all over the place nowadays, haven't they? I don't think they're that far behind the times even out there,' she laughed. 'Anyway, the villages along the trail are bound to have reception and its high up there too don't forget.'

'That's true.' She recalled reading that Minions was said to be the highest village in Cornwall. She would make sure to check her phone later when Jodie's mum dropped them there.

'You'll be fine along the trail. Just don't go wandering off into the middle of the moor somewhere. Anyway, I'm going up to get changed now, then I'll drop you off at the station on the way to the supermarket. My shift doesn't start until ten. Okay?'

'Okay mum.'

Thirty minutes later Maddie was holding the backpack by both straps and heaving it into the boot of her mother's car, surprised by her own strength, thinking it wasn't really cheating by using her knee to help kick it up over the bottom of the boot. Earlier that morning, on Jodie's advice, she had gotten it onto her back, yanked the front straps until everything felt nice and tight, then jumped up and down on the spot, feeling a bit silly watching her reflection in the mirror though. And if nothing rattled, fell off, or flapped about and the pack felt comfortable, staying snug against her body like it was supposed to, then she had done everything right and it should still be there one mile into the hike or even ten miles later.

'Proper planning prevents poor performance.' Jodie had said, the remark making Maddie laugh aloud at the time from the wise old head on young nineteen-year-old shoulders dishing out such sensible advice. Now that her backpack had passed muster, she knew she was in safe hands with her friend.

She had known Jodie since secondary school. They had both turned eleven when they'd first met at Poltair Community College in Cornwall, before her mum and her had moved away to Plymouth when she'd turned seventeen and a half. Maddie's grandparents lived in Plymouth and her mum had always wanted to live closer to them, especially as they were getting on in years and found the regular trip to Cornwall to see them not as easy anymore. The one-way trip alone could take at least fifty-minutes but could easily extend to over an hour if the traffic was heavy leaving the city or they encountered roadworks on the way down. It could take even longer in the summer months when families took to the busy motorways and headed for the South West. Although the main route into

Cornwall had been improved over the years, it hadn't gone far enough as the sheer volume of visitors nearly always guaranteed a long wait in a traffic jam somewhere.

They had been on the housing association swap scheme for two years before one suddenly came up for grabs: an older couple wanted to retire down to Cornwall. It couldn't have come at a better time for them, and her mum had jumped at the chance to swop, settling in Plymouth a full two months before Maddie turned eighteen and was due to start her university course.

Jodie had always been the practical, outdoors type, not academically gifted like she was, much more at home helping her parents out on the farm she'd grown up on, playing net ball and hockey at school or just riding her horse around in the back field every opportunity she got. Despite their different personalities, they had become good friends (sometimes opposites attract) and remained that way throughout most of their school years. They had agreed to keep in touch after she'd moved to Plymouth and unlike most people they did, texting or phoning each other every week or so with all the latest news and gossip. Last November, Jodie had crossed the Tamar bridge that separated Cornwall from Devon (a short fifty-minute journey by car) and they'd met up for lunch in the city and a girly chat, before hitting the shops to do their

Christmas shopping.

It was in the little café, over burgers and chips and hot coffee, that Jodie came up with the idea of the pair of them taking a little hiking trip around Bodmin Moor next summer. It had been thrown out there; a suggestion, a maybe, something to think about; she hadn't expected an instant decision. Jodie couldn't have hidden her delight even if she'd wanted to when Maddie had said she loved the idea. She hadn't seen Cornwall in over a year, suddenly realising how much she'd missed the tranquillity and rugged countryside, and the fresh air would do her the world of good. Jodie had given her the perfect opportunity to recharge her batteries before the new term started, to forget about studying for a while and the hustle and bustle of life in the city. She was really looking forward to it.

The car pulled into an empty drop off space outside the entrance, arriving thirty minutes before the train was due to depart. Her daughter had plenty of time to get her ticket and find the right platform.

Maddie heaved her backpack out of the boot, with slightly more of a struggle this time.

'You need a hand with that?'

'I got it,' she said, dumping it on the ground. Now for the part she'd practised earlier. Bending her legs, she slipped an arm through one strap and bundled it onto her back, before sliding her other arm through the strap opposite. Now, that wasn't difficult she told herself.

Her mum smiled proudly. 'Looks like you've done that before?'

'I have,' Maddie admitted. 'In my room about ten times. Didn't want everyone thinking I was a complete novice or make an idiot of myself trying to get the damn thing on my back.'

'Well, you managed to fool me Maddie so nobody will suspect a thing. I'm sure.'

'Good.'

'Don't forget to phone, won't you? Or at least send me a text,' she said, throwing her arms around her briefly. Although mother and daughter were close, neither of them were overly affectionate physically.

'Don't worry, I'll keep in touch.' Maddie yanked hard on the straps, pulling the pack tighter into her back. It felt nice and secure now.

'You've got your phone, haven't you?'

Maddie slid a hand into the back pocket of her jeans. 'Right here,' she said, showing her it. It hadn't hurt to check; just in case. 'Better go get my ticket mum.'

'Okay then. Have a great time and say hello to Jodie and her mum for me.'

'Will do, see you in a few days then.' Maddie

turned and headed towards the entrance. The automatic doors slid open when she got close enough, but she didn't go in just then. She turned and waved. 'If I see the Beast of Bodmin, I'll send you a photo.'

Her mum was opening the car door. 'Be sure you do,' she laughed, waving back at her. 'And watch out for the creepy crawlies!'

She waited until Maddie disappeared through the sliding doors, before getting into her car and driving away from the station.

TWO

It wasn't a big terminal; not for a city. Four ticket booths, two with the blinds down and two open, a single row of red plastic bucket seats bolted to the floor running the length of the wall to her right; a couple of monitors overhead showing arrivals and departures. The hot drinks machine in the corner looked oddly out of place Maddie thought. Not that she could make a direct comparison. She'd never been to the likes of Manchester, Birmingham or London, places that could swallow you up by their sheer size alone and make you feel isolated and lonely with its multiple platforms, rows of ticket booths, cafes, restaurants, not to mention the swarm of commuters rushing madly about with blank, robotic expressions on their faces. And the constant train announcements; '*ding dong... the train arriving at platform...'* Half the time you couldn't hear what they were saying anyway above the noise of the trains.

But to Maddie, this *was* big. When the doors behind her had thudded shut, sealing off the bustle from outside, she had stood there, a touch self-conscious with that pack on her back, looking back through the window, watching the car drive away from her. Suddenly she'd felt a little bit lonely, tinged though with a sense of excitement for what lay ahead of her. She was on her own now.

She went over to the nearest ticket booth and stood peering through the glass that separated her and the twenties something woman sitting inside. Partly because this booth was closer, but mainly because she didn't like the look of the middle-aged man occupying the other one; he had shifty looking eyes; she'd caught him running them over a couple of young women when they bent over to retrieve their coffee from the machine. What a sleaze Maddie thought. Why was it always the older one's she caught doing that and not the good looking guys her own age?

'Can I help?' the twenties something woman asked, looking neat and official in her white blouse and dark blue blazer, a little badge depicting a train pinned to her lapel, reinforcing the fact she worked for the railway.

'PLEASE SPEAK HERE' was printed on the

glass in white letters. She leaned close to the speak holes beneath the notice. 'One ticket to St Austell please!'

'Single or return?' the twenties something woman smiled.

'Oh – return please.' Maddie pulled a canvas wallet from her back pocket.

'That'll be nine pound fifty,' she said and started punching keys on a machine on the counter beside her.

Maddie pulled a credit card from her wallet, holding it playfully between the fingers of both hands, while the twenties something woman printed up her ticket. She glanced to her right and caught the shifty man in the other booth looking at her, then casually lower his gaze as if to disguise any hint of impropriety. Sleaze, she thought again, wondering if he was married and how his poor wife might feel if she knew how he passed the time while he was working.

Her ticket was slid towards her, and she did the same with her credit card, nudging it under the gap beneath the glass. Picking it up, she examined it to ensure she'd been given the right one.

'Thank you,' the twenties something woman said, returning her card. 'That's platform two, the nine twenty-one to St Austell.'

Maddie kept the ticket out and shoved her wallet back in her jeans. 'Thanks for your help'.

'You're welcome. Have a nice journey.'

The twenties something woman had been so polite and helpful that Maddie half thought about leaning forward and whispering a message: *'Watch him over there – he's a bit of a letch.'* But she probably knew that already.

She turned from the ticket booth and checked her watch. Twenty minutes until her train. Before going through the station, she thought about grabbing a coffee from the machine, but when she saw the man with the shifty eyes still giving her the occasional glance, she headed for the platform deciding coffee could wait and she'd buy one later when she boarded the train.

Maddie crossed the ticket area, ignoring the hot drinks machine and the letch in the booth, following a woman in front of her, watching her every move as she negotiated a turn style ticket gate. When the woman went through, she fed her ticket into the slot, and grabbed the returned portion that slid out the other end. The barrier clunked open and she passed through, making her way along the short underpass that would lead to the platforms above. The one she wanted was up a short flight of steps that branched off the passageway, and she climbed them forcefully, clutching the central handrail, the backpack feeling ominously heavier the higher she went. There weren't many hills where she was going, was there?

she mused, trying to recall if Jodie had ever mentioned anything about hills, her mind so preoccupied now with finding her platform she couldn't be sure if Jodie had mentioned it or not.

She reached the top step and saw platform two. The train was already sitting there: 'Great First Western' in white letters emblazoned along its side, waiting for the driver to start its engine and the guard to arrive and give the signal when it was safe to pull away. For the moment, it was silent.

Ambling over to the platform she dumped her backpack on the ground, leaning it against one of the four plastic seats that nobody was sitting on. There were a handful of people waiting here, spread out across the length of the platform as if they needed to give each other some space. A middle-aged couple were sitting in a waiting room that resembled a bus that hadn't had its cab or wheels added to it yet. The woman was engrossed in a paperback and the man was reading a newspaper.

A young mother with a toddler in a buggy was standing the other side of the seats where she'd placed her backpack. She was shouting at her son, maybe eight years old Maddie guessed, who was running up and down the platform making aeroplane sounds as he weaved a slalom around the bemused looking passengers. The mother glanced over at Maddie and smiled nervously.

'Kids eh.'

Maddie smiled back. 'Weren't we all once.'

'He can be a little bugger at times,' she said, glad Maddie hadn't shown disapproval at her son's behaviour. Her nervous look faded. 'Drives me nuts sometimes, does Tommy.'

'I bet he does,' Maddie laughed.

'Tommy!' she hollered. The boy had gone further down the platform and was peering through one of the train windows, too close to the edge. Quickly she wheeled the buggy round and headed after him. 'Get back Tommy – come here this minute!' The toddler in the buggy started to screech.

Kids eh, Maddie thought, remembering the mothers remark. It wasn't for her though – not for a long time yet. She'd studied hard to get into university, only just getting the grades she needed to gain entry; having babies and a relationship were the last thing on her mind right now. Although there were plenty of available guys at the university – some of them cute too she'd noticed – she'd resisted the temptation to get into anything serious that would distract her from her studying. There would be plenty of time for that after she gained her degree and hopefully a half decent career, her ambition fuelled in part by her mother's encouragement during her school years and her own acute awareness of the hardships they'd both endured due to lack of money and the fact her mum had been a single parent to her. When her mum had met Steve, a fellow co-worker at the supermarket she worked for, Maddie thought things were finally looking up now. He had seemed a nice enough man when mum had brought him home for tea one afternoon and introduced him to her. They had dated for over four months and her mum was happy, until she discovered from a friend the awful truth that Steve was in fact already married to someone else and was just using her for a bit on the side. Her mum had been devastated. If losing her husband early in their marriage hadn't been bad enough, this had been a cruel kick in the teeth and it was no wonder she had shied away from getting involved with anyone else. And although Steve and her mum worked in different departments – he was in stock control and she manned the check outs – he even had the gall to remain there after it all came out, pretending nothing had happened but only causing her further distress. At first, her sheer anger had clouded any feelings of betrayal and she thought she could deal with it, hoping guilt might force him to do the decent thing and resign from his position. He was in the wrong, not her. But Steve just weathered the storm, keeping his head down, avoiding her as much as possible in the vain and arrogant hope that it might all blow over. He wasn't going anywhere. Eventually, the gossip, the humiliation, the guarded whispers she became increasingly aware of between her fellow workers, became too much to handle and she left the company after finding a job with a rival supermarket chain. Now that he was out of her life, the wounds slowly began to heal and it was only a matter of a month or so before mum was back to her normal self again.

Further along the platform, the opposite direction the mother had gone, she spotted the familiar shape of a vending machine, grabbed her pack and headed towards it, hoping it wasn't a soft drinks machine. She needed caffeine. When she got there, she saw a sheet of paper taped across the front: 'OUT OF ORDER' greeting her in big red letters. 'Typical,' she muttered.

'Ding – dong.' Then a female voice announced. 'The next train to depart from platform two will be the nine twenty-one to Penzance, calling at Liskeard...'

Maddie found herself paying close attention to the stations called out, despite the fact she'd watched them scrolling across a monitor only minutes before. Partly because it was human nature to worry about getting on the wrong train, mainly because it was something to listen to while she waited.

'...Bodmin Parkway, Par, St Austell, Truro, Redruth, Camborne, St Erth and Penzance.'

Three stops until St Austell. But she knew that already.

More people were arriving on the platform. Some had gotten caught up in traffic, some hadn't allowed enough time to get to the station and others had simply lost track of time sitting in the stations café eating hot toast and drinking coffee. Maddie hoped the train wouldn't be too busy and that she could find herself a seat, acutely aware – from her friends at university who regularly used the railway to get home for the holidays – that it could be standing room only at certain busy periods of the year. She remembered some of them complaining about how they had been forced to sit on the floor or stand in the aisle for the whole journey. Although student railcards relieved the pain from some of the highest ticket prices in Europe, it would be nice to get a seat for a change.

Maddie was relieved to hear the train thunder into life and a guard appeared as if from nowhere, flag in his hand. Soon, she might be able to get herself some caffeine she thought, and with a few short strides she was standing by the door waiting for it to slide open, backpack near her shins and with a handful of commuters queuing around her.

Minutes later and she had found herself a window seat having already stowed her pack in the luggage compartment at the end of the carriage. The train wasn't that busy for the time of the year

Maddie realised, noticing quite a few empty seats in the carriage she occupied. But then, it was early yet and most people holidaying in Cornwall would make the journey by car, families heading for the plentiful caravan parks or family resorts dotted around the coastal regions. Others, mostly singles or young couples, would head for the seaside towns like Newquay, spending the day surfing or lazing on the beach, before hitting the towns pubs, nightclubs and restaurants. That sort of holiday had never appealed to her. Like most students, she enjoyed partying with her friends and having a few drinks, but not to excess, and couldn't stand music so loud it drowned out the person speaking right next to you. All too often, and typical of many metropolitan areas up and down the country, the lure of cheap drink and the availability of drugs – especially the new designer types – could turn an otherwise fun night out into a drunken pub crawl with people fighting or throwing up in the gutter. It wasn't her idea of a holiday at all or Jodie's either.

Jodie, she thought, and picked up her phone from the table separating her from the empty seat opposite. A thin paperback lay there: 'A Guide to Bodmin Moor.' She had found it quite by accident whilst rummaging through a bargain bin in a book store in Plymouth, hidden amongst the short fiction romance novels and the 'do it yourself' guides. It was half price, giving her the same gratification from discovering a designer garment at a ridiculously cheap price in one of the many second hand clothes shops and charity outlets that seemed to have sprung up in recent years. Sometimes mum would join her on one of her bargain hunts around the city and it would always turn into a little contest between the pair of them to see who could grab the best deal.

A whistle shrilled outside, followed by the bleeping of the electronic doors, signifying they were now remotely locked. Moments later and Maddie felt a sudden jolt as the train lurched forward, picking up speed gradually and crawling out of the station.

She sent a text message to Jodie, telling her she was just leaving Plymouth, and all being well would be arriving in St Austell in an hour or so. Not long after a message came back. 'Great, see you soon x.'

Once the train had left Plymouth, a voice came over the intercom telling her the buffet car was now open for drinks and hot and cold snacks, and she wasted no time in heading to the front of the train where it was situated, leaving her book on the table to let people know the seat was occupied.

Maddie made her way down through the carriages, passing the passengers sitting in their seats, some staring blankly through the window, some reading, others listening through earphones that weren't up to the job – or turned up too high – as she could hear garbled music, kids swiping fingers on tablets and smartly dressed business people hunched over laptops with a look of concentration on their faces as they tried catching up on some work before arriving at the office. Two seats ahead she saw the mother and her two kids she had spoken to earlier, the toddler sitting happily on her lap now and Tommy in the seat beside her scribbling with some crayons on a colouring book. She smiled at Maddie as she went past.

Before opening the door to the buffet car, she stopped in the walkway that connected with the carriage behind and peered curiously through the window at the panoramic view that now presented itself. The train was lumbering over the Royal Albert Bridge which spanned the river Tamar between Plymouth and Cornwall. Against the shimmering blue backdrop, she could see the flotilla of little boats and yachts glinting in the sunlight as they bobbed about in the river below. It was a long way down, Maddie thought. In a matter of minutes the bridge would be behind them as they crossed into Cornwall through the town of Saltash, also known as the gateway to Cornwall.

Returning with a much-needed coffee, she settled into her seat again, and peered out the window, her eyes registering only the blur streaking past as they focused on nothing in particular. The coffee was okay. It wasn't the best she'd ever had but it was hot and sweet and provided much needed caffeine, but she had to sip it carefully though or risk burning her mouth and tongue.

'Tickets please!' The conductor was making his way down the carriage.

Maddie took it out and when he reached her seat he examined it briefly before punching her ticket. 'Thank you,' he said. His measured tone accompanied just the hint of a smile as he passed the ticket back, before moving on methodically to the other passengers behind her.

Maddie picked up her book, opened it at the turned down corner, and started to read from where she had left off yesterday. It was crammed with useful information for either the casual visitor wanting to take in some of the moors historic sights, or the more energetic sightseer wanting to explore its many walking routes and off the beat trails. There was plenty to see on the moor: underground caverns, Cornwall's famous coaching house Jamaica Inn that sat high on Bodmin Moor, Dozmary Pool, the supposed resting place of King Arthur's sword Excalibur as well as numerous ancient standing stone circles and quoits. Maddie knew they'd only have time to explore some of them during the three-day hike and both girls had discussed the possibility of perhaps returning at a later date to explore what they had missed.

A male voice crackled from the intercom. 'The train is now approaching Bodmin Parkway. Bodmin Parkway is the next station stop.'

The train slowed as it approached the station, reducing to no more than an amble as the platform appeared alongside. As it creaked to a halt Maddie took her eyes off the page and looked out at the people waiting there to board. There weren't many. A couple wearing jeans and tee shirts, rucksacks slung over their shoulders and a better dressed middle aged man carrying a brown duffel bag.

She went back to her book, then decided she had better go to the toilet first before starting a new page. It was two seats behind, the green light above the doorway indicating it was vacant. She grabbed her phone, leaving her book again, and headed for the loo.

Once inside the cramped space, Maddie put the seat down and pulled down her jeans and knickers, squatting an inch or so over the seat, hands on her knees. She didn't sit on public toilets; not if she could help it. Sometimes, if the seat looked grubby, she would place some toilet paper down, but this one looked like it had been cleaned recently. The 'DO NOT FLUSH WHEN IN STATION' sign she'd seen stayed firmly in her mind, and she wondered what the consequences might be for not observing it. She wasn't about to find out though. After she'd finished, Maddie washed her hands in the tiny sink and took the opportunity to refresh her face with cold water. Although it had just turned ten, it was already beginning to feel a little warm and Maddie knew another fine day lay ahead of her. When the train started moving again she flushed the loo and left the cubicle.

She had an outdoors look. You could tell by the ruddy complexion, the skin wrinkled and leathery, partly because of old age but mainly because its owner had weathered the elements for more than a few years. That she'd done her fair share of manual work was evident by the gnarled hands and sinewy fingers laced in her lap. Her brown eyes looked tired, lacking the sparkle of youth, the whites a pale-yellow now. She had to be at least eighty. That was Maddie's first thought anyway when she returned to her seat and saw the woman with the silver-grey hair sitting in the seat opposite hers, peering out through the window.

Maddie wondered where she had come from as she hadn't seen her standing on the platform at the last station. Or had she just missed her? Perhaps she'd been on the train all along and had simply decided to move to a different seat. Not that it mattered.

As Maddie approached she saw the old woman was wearing a smart pleated skirt that covered her knees but wasn't ankle length and a cream coloured blouse that was buttoned all the way to her neck. The green unbuttoned cardigan on top made Maddie think she must be uncomfortably warm in all that, before realising that the elderly were much more prone to the cold than her nineteen-year-old body would ever be.

They shared a polite smile as Maddie took her seat again and it was only a matter of a minute or so before the woman spoke.

'Lovely weather we're having,' she said cheerfully.

'Beautiful isn't it.' Maddie couldn't agree more. There wasn't a cloud in the sky, the early morning sunlight already casting a bright golden hue over the undulating landscape and for a moment, Maddie felt a strange sense of detachment from the world outside as she became lost in the rhythm of the train as it ran over the tracks beneath her. It seemed almost surreal. She took a sip of her coffee which she noticed was still too hot and settled back in her seat.

The old lady opened a carpet bag that was sitting on the seat beside her, rummaged inside and pulled out a big handful of knitting. Placing it in her lap, she untangled the wool before taking the needles in both hands and starting to knit, the dexterity of her fingers taking Maddie by surprise. She made it look effortless.

The woman noticed Maddie's interest. 'Oh – just takes lots of practice that's all.'

'You make it look easy.'

The woman smiled appreciatively. 'I've been doing it for years dear. So long in fact I can do it with my eyes closed.' She gave a short laugh.

'Did your mother teach you?'

'Oh yes, and *her* mother taught her. Girls would have been encouraged back then, especially so during the First World War when there was a shortage of socks in particular.'

'Socks?'

'Yes, the dreaded trench foot dear. Played havoc with their feet you know.'

'Yes, of course,' Maddie acknowledged, remembering her history now, and how the wet and cold conditions of the trenches had resulted in thousands of troops suffering from the affliction. To combat the condition, they had been issued with three pairs of socks and instructed to change them at least twice daily. Wooden duck boards were later introduced and placed along the trenches which helped eradicate the problem.

'And did you know that knitting patterns were even issued so that people could make gloves and balaclavas for the soldiers and sailors during winter? Aside from anything else it gave people at home a sense of contributing to the war effort.'

'I never knew that.' Maddie said with genuine

surprise as the old woman continued.

'I'd watch her for ages, fascinated, just like you're doing now. After pestering the life out of her she eventually gave in, sat me down one day and taught me how to do it. It was tricky to begin with and I remember thinking I'd never get the hang of it. Getting up to speed was the hardest part. Fourteen I was, if my memory serves.'

'I'd be all fingers and thumbs,' Maddie confessed, vaguely recalling her granny knitting years ago when she was a little girl but unable to fully appreciate it at the time. It was obviously not as common a practice nowadays and she wondered if the skill had been resigned now to the enthusiast hobbyist or those with plenty of time on their hands.

'Well – so would I if I had to use one of those.' She looked accusingly at Maddie's phone resting on the book.

'How anyone can use them one handed and hold a conversation with the person next to them is beyond me.'

Maddie grinned, impressed by the woman's wit. 'Yes – I'm guilty of that.'

'What is it they call it...? The old lady had to think for a second. 'Multitasking – isn't it?

'That's right,' exclaimed Maddie, surprised she'd even heard the term, let alone knew what it meant. 'Is that a scarf your making?'

'Yes dear, it is.'

'It's lovely,' Maddie said, admiring the intricate detail of the colourful material that draped over the old woman's knees.

'You're probably wondering why a silly old woman like me would be knitting a scarf in the middle of summer.'

'No, of course not,' Maddie said sincerely, although she did wonder. 'I expect it takes ages to make something as pretty as that with that zig zag pattern and the different colours too.'

The compliment had warmed her towards the young woman. 'I give them to my family every Christmas. There's quite a few of them you know so I need to start early you see.'

'That's a lovely thought.'

'Well – when you get to my age you've run out of ideas by then. I never have a clue what to get them anymore and I don't get around the shops like I used to. The arthritis in my hip has seen to that.'

'No – I'm sure,' Maddie concurred, detecting no hint of self-pity in the woman's voice and marvelling at how she managed to cope with the difficulties train travel might present to someone of her age and frailty.

'I see you have a book there on Bodmin Moor.'

Maddie glanced at the cover. 'Yes – it's a good read,' she said, touching it with her fingers. 'Have you ever visited the area?'

There was a distinct pause before the old lady replied.

'Oh...that was a very long time ago now...' Maddie saw the wistful look in her eyes. '...way back before you were born dear. I suppose it hasn't changed that much over the years though.'

'No – I don't think it has,' Maddie agreed, the windswept craggy landscape she'd seen in old as well as more recent photographs virtually identical as she recalled. The only real change it seemed was the addition of modern signage to the narrow roads and hamlets that predominately skirted around the edge of the moor.

'Are you holidaying in Cornwall?'

'Only for a few days. Backpacking around Bodmin Moor on the Copper Moor Trail.'

The woman raised her eyebrows. 'I've never heard of that one. Is it new?'

'You could say that, compared to the age of the moor itself, but it's been around for a number of years now and is very popular with walkers. The trail runs for sixty miles right around the edge of the moor –'

'– sixty miles! My goodness me...'

Maddie smiled awkwardly. 'Probably invented for the tourists like me,' she joked, not wishing to dampen the woman's surprised delight by revealing to her she wasn't walking that far. 'But I grew up in Cornwall, before moving to Plymouth a year ago, so I suppose I shouldn't call myself a tourist, should I?

'You were born in Cornwall?'

'Truro. The Royal Cornwall Hospital. Then mum and I lived in St Austell right up until I was nearly eighteen.'

'Well then – your Cornish through and through, aren't you dear? so you shouldn't think of yourself as a tourist at all,' the old woman admonished her.

Maddie gave a short smile. 'I guess not.'

'Anyway, getting back to the hiking trip you were telling me about...' The old lady looked directly at Maddie. 'You should be okay on a proper trail but the moor has its own hidden dangers and the weather can be very unpredictable too. And before you know it a mist can come down in no time. But I suppose you already know about all that?'

Maddie nodded. The book did say the weather could change rapidly on the moor and it was always advisable to carry a map and compass as many of the paths were unmarked. It was easy to get lost. But that was Jodie's area of expertise. She didn't know the first thing about using a map or compass, not that they would need them anyway.

She picked up her coffee, noting it had cooled and took a couple of longer sips, before hearing the familiar voice over the intercom announcing the next stop. 'The train is now approaching Par. Par will be the next station stop.'

Two people got on. It seemed that the further they travelled into Cornwall the less passengers there were waiting on the tiny platforms. But that's what Maddie loved about the county, the tranquillity and idyllic pace of life a stark contrast to the bustling city she had left behind not more than an hour ago.

St Austell was only minutes away now. She waited for the announcement, before grabbing her things and standing up from her seat.

The woman looked up from her knitting. 'Your stop dear?'

'St Austell, yes.'

She moved to the aisle, the train slowing to a crawl now as it approached the station, the carriage jerking sideways so that Maddie had to clutch the seats either side.

Looking at the old woman she asked: 'Have you got much further to go yourself?'

'Oh – not too far now dear,' she replied, peering up at her. 'Not too far at all.'

'Well – enjoy the rest of your journey,' Maddie said. 'Bye now.'

'Bye dear.'

Maddie started making her way down the carriage. Preoccupied now with retrieving her backpack from the rack and getting off the train in time she vaguely registered the old lady's parting comment a few seats back.

'Take care now dear – both of you.'

THREE

Jodie recognised her friend the instant she got off the train, the backpack looped over one shoulder making her stand out amongst the few people that were milling about on the platform. Some, just like her, were here to greet friends or relatives, others waiting to board and travel on to Redruth or the last station in Penzance.

'Over here Maddie!' She waved excitedly at the figure making her way from the far end of the platform where her carriage had stopped.

They hugged each other, Jodie pulling away and looking down at Maddie's feet. 'I see you've got your walking boots, you're going to need them,' she teased. It was the first time she'd seen her wearing boots instead of the smart trainers she normally wore and they looked comically big on her feet.

'Funny ha ha,' Maddie said, screwing her face up, noting the mischievous glint in Jodie's green eyes and realising her attempt to match her friend's wit had fallen short as usual. There were other more obvious differences between the pair of them. Jodie's hair was curly brown and unkempt, her bigger frame and ruddy complexion making her appear every inch the typical farmer's daughter. She was a good two inches taller too.

'Come on, mum's waiting in the car.' Jodie led her friend through the tiny station and into the parking area just the other side which shared space with the local bus company that ferried passengers back and forth between the numerous villages and the historic market town of St Austell. As Maddie stepped out from the confines of the station, she took time to take in the familiar surroundings that didn't seem to have changed one bit, and she felt an overwhelming sense of comfort that one might experience from coming home again after a long absence.

As they approached the car Jodie shooed away the lone seagull boldly scavenging around the parking space, an ice cream wrapper stuck to its beak. It flew off and landed on top of a waiting bus, its head twitching as it scoured the station looking for scraps of food.

'Nothing much changes around here,' Maddie remarked, amused by the seagull's antics as it now perched on top of a rubbish bin trying to balance itself as it leaned over to rummage through the contents.

'The flying rats haven't, that's for sure. They're a real nuisance nowadays. I swear they're getting bolder by the day.'

Maddie recalled the time she'd visited the tiny fishing village of Mevagissey with her mum during the summer and how a seagull had swooped down and grabbed a pasty right out of her hands. At the time, she didn't know whether to laugh or cry. Cheeky buggers! It didn't help that some people continued to feed them leftover chips or pasty crusts, ignoring the signs placed by the local council - around the coastal areas frequented by tourists – not to feed the seagulls. And it wasn't uncommon for residents to place their household waste in seagull proof bags to stop the blighters ripping them open and strewing rubbish all over the road.

The fifty-minute drive to Minions village was uneventful, more so for the driver than the passengers she carried. The two girls chatted non-stop the whole way, Jodie looking over her shoulder now and again to Maddie in the back, her backpack sitting beside her as the car wasn't big enough to fit two of them into the tiny boot. They talked about the adventure that lay ahead of them; how much they were looking forward to roughing it in the great outdoors and sleeping under the stars. They both laughed when Jodie said: 'what you going to do if you find a grass snake in your sleeping bag?' The mood changed when Jodie's mum wittily asked them if there were mosquitos on the moor, and had they thought to pack any insect repellent, and she waited for the stupefied look to appear on the girls faces before allowing herself to laugh aloud at her own joke.

They chatted about the weather, the points of interest on the trail and all the photos they should take. Sometimes the driver managed to get a word in, with a 'How does it feel to be back in Cornwall again Maddie?' or 'How's you mum doing? Is she still working at the supermarket?' Or 'How did she find university?' They talked about the Beast of Bodmin, a phantom wild cat that was supposed to roam the moor, and what would they do if they came across it. Take a photo first because no one would believe them, then run like hell, Maddie said. And so it went on, until they ran out of things to talk about around their forthcoming hiking trip, and the conversation turned to normal things like the weather and would they be able to get something to eat at the village as it would nearly be lunch time when they arrived. Jodie said there was a little café there that she had seen on the Copper Moor Trail web page. A hot pasty and a cup of coffee would go down well before they set off on the first eight-mile leg to the village of St Neot.

The busy main arteries soon became a distant memory as the car snaked its way along winding country roads, passing through picturesque villages or tiny thatched hamlets that looked like they belonged on a picture postcard, the sort of place discovered quite by accident by the occasional visitor who would delight in its charm. Once or twice they had to pull over in narrow lanes to allow the odd car or tractor through, the drivers always giving a polite nod or a wave of appreciation as they passed. Unlike the city, Maddie thought, with its frustrated drivers blasting their horns at each other or shouting abuse simply because they'd got out of bed the wrong side that morning.

'Not far now,' the driver said, as she went over the cattle grid a little too fast, the car bouncing and tyres juddering.

As far as the eye could see, rugged moorland stretched out all around them, home to the sheep, ponies and cattle that roamed across the moor including the narrow road they were now crawling along. The village of Minions was just up ahead.

'This place is more popular than ever now,' Jodie's mum said. 'Ever since that Minions movie was released last year. Once people found out there was a village with the same name they've been coming here in droves.'

'They put a new sign up too, didn't they?' Jodie

said. 'Outside the village?'

Her mum smiled in amusement. 'To celebrate the film, yes. It was a picture of the characters themselves with the slogan welcome to minions. Very popular too. But the council took it down for safety reasons because they said too many people were stopping alongside it to have their pictures taken.'

'That's a shame,' Maddie said. 'I'd liked to have seen that.'

'I know,' Jodie's mum said, looking at Maddie in her rear-view mirror. 'And it did help put the village on the map too. Some of the locals were outraged when they took it down apparently, especially the business owners who benefited from the extra tourism...'

Just then she was forced to stop the car, relieved she had kept her speed down.

'Come one buddie, your holding us up,' Jodie scolded the sheep that was standing nonchalantly in the road with its head turned their way. Maddie leaned forward to see what all the fuss was about and her face brightened. It was obvious the animals here were quite used to cars and sightseers on this section of the moor. Taking its time, the sheep crossed the narrow road and joined the others grazing by the roadside.

The road ahead clear now, the car picked up speed as it passed a lonely looking sign that proclaimed, 'Welcome to MINIONS. Please drive carefully.'

The car swung into the already busy car park. No tarmac here Maddie saw; just a rough area of ground that looked out of place next to the moorland, as if someone had come along with a digger and taken a slice right out of it and then covered it with gravel. People were already out of their cars, cameras in hand, some attaching leads to excited dogs looking forward to a walk, mindful of the notice 'Please Keep Dogs Under Strict Control.' It wouldn't have been the first time a careless dog owner had forgotten to attach a lead and incurred the wrath of the local farmer when his sheep were being chased across the moor.

Backpacks dumped on the ground, they took time to stretch their limbs before taking in the barren landscape and the handful of white washed houses just to their right that formed part of the village. Maddie laughed when Jodie said it reminded her of that film she had seen about two American backpackers on the Yorkshire moors who had been attacked by a werewolf, but she couldn't remember the name of it. Maddie did. It was called 'An American Werewolf in London.' All three of them shared briefly in the laughter, before Jodie's mum reminded them she would pick them up at St Breward – the last leg of their hike – on Monday afternoon and to ring her to confirm what

45

time they would be there. They waved at the car until it went out of sight, then stood in the carpark deciding what they should do first.

Maddie pulled out her phone. Just one bar was greyed out, the remainder bright green. The signal was good and Mum had been right.

Jodie got her map out. 'The Hurlers should be around here somewhere...'

'The standing stones – right?' Maddie slipped her phone back in the rear pocket of her jeans.

'Yes,' Jodie said, facing a dirt track that led onto the moor and disappeared a short distance away over a slight crest. 'That path should lead us straight to them. Want to take a look first and then grab some lunch? It's not very far.'

'Good idea. I'm starving,' Maddie said, keen to take some snaps of the bronze age circle she had read about before getting something to eat in the village. She recalled from her guide book the legend about a group of local men who had been playing a game named 'hurling' on the Sabbath and how they had been turned to stone as a punishment by a humourless deity. Although it was a fascinating story, Maddie took the mainstream view that it probably had some astronomical significance, but it was good for the tourism, which contributed to a large part of the Cornish economy.

The track was narrow, forcing them to go single file to avoid tripping or twisting an ankle in the thick tussocks either side. The bigger girl was in front. The crest was a two-minute walk away, the slight incline proving easy underfoot. This wasn't too bad, Maddie thought, encouraged by how light the weight on her back felt and recalling how heavy it had seemed back home when she'd tried lifting the dead weight straight off the floor. She wondered if she would be feeling the same at the end of the day though after having put in more than a few miles.

Jodie pulled up as she reached the top of the crest. 'There they are,' she exclaimed.

Maddie came along side, and because of her elevated position could see that the stones covered a much larger area than she had anticipated. She idly imagined if it had been dusk now, without the shadows they cast against the grass, they might appear almost domino like as they stood upright against the bleak landscape.

There were three separate stone circles, spread out in a straight line across the moor one behind the other, the middle and largest an elliptical shape, only the outer ones forming circles. Over one hundred and sixty metres in length it was the only known example of a stone circle linear in the whole of England, Maddie recalled from her guide book. They were overlooked, a mile away, by a granite tor known as the Cheesewring, a formation of smooth oval shaped stones that in the photo she thought looked like pancakes stacked precariously on top of one another. And although giving the appearance of having being man-made they were a completely natural formation caused by weather erosion.

The girls saw a small group of sightseers had already gathered there. They wandered amongst the stones, touching them curiously with their hands or stood posing in front of them as they had their pictures taken, the few sheep and horses grazing close by at ease with the interlopers provided they kept their distance and didn't try approaching them.

They started off again, stopping to take a photo when they got close enough to frame them all, soon joining the small group already there and admiring the ancient bronze age monoliths.

A woman walking her dog agreed to take a photo of the pair of them, and the girls grinned inanely at the lens as they stood proudly in front of one of the bigger stones. The Hurlers weren't as tall as they'd expected them to be, most of them not much higher than either of them. They weren't in the same league as Stonehenge in Wiltshire, Jodie said. She had been there a few years back and remembered how the large structure towered way above her. Nearly thirty-feet high, she recalled someone telling her at the time. But despite the fact the Hurlers weren't as impressive in size, they were unique in their own way and they could only wonder at the importance they must have held to the bronze age people who had transported them here across difficult terrain. Maddie had read in the guide that there had once been a stone path that ran right through the middle of the circles – now overgrown by grassland – and historians had speculated it might have served as a processional route for some sort of ancient ceremony that had gone unrecorded and lost now in the passage of time. The theory was as good as any, but visitors and archaeologists alike could only speculate as to the true meaning behind the existence of the strange circles.

The girls made the short journey across the moor to visit the Pipers, a pair of standing stones that according to folk lore represented musicians. Maddie flicked through the guide as they ambled towards them, hoping to gain further insight as to their meaning. Near Land's End, Maddie now read, stood a circle of nineteen standing stones called the Merry Maidens who were distracted by the playing from the Pipers a quarter of a mile away and strayed into a field to dance to the music. A thunderbolt struck the Maidens, turning them to stone and the Pipers were frozen to the spot for the sin of playing on the Sabbath. It all sounded very romantic, Maddie thought, as she took a picture of Jodie standing in front of them and grinning like a

Cheshire cat.

Eventually, when they tired of taking snaps and realised it was lunch time and they were feeling hungrier now, they made the short journey back across the moor in search of the little café in the village.

They discovered it nestled amongst the quaint white washed houses, some proudly displaying neatly kept window boxes or hanging baskets over flowing with brightly coloured flowers. If it hadn't been for the little 'OPEN' sign resting against the window in front of the café style voile curtain or the sandwich board placed out front, they might have mistaken it for one of the cottages alongside and walked past missing it altogether.

The smell of hot pasties and sausage rolls, mixed with an even stronger aroma of freshly ground coffee wafted over them when Maddie opened the door, a bell ringing over the doorframe signalling their arrival. It wasn't that busy yet and they had their choice of seats, opting for one in the corner where they could place their backpacks behind them and out of the way of other customers.

'I'm definitely having coffee.' Maddie took one of the menus wedged between condiment pots.

'Me too,' Jodie said, settling into her seat and then pulling her chair closer to the smallish round table.

The menu was a single sheet; food on one side and drinks on the other and Maddie was surprised when she saw the variety of snacks available from a café that could easily have been mistaken from the outside for a village tea room.

'I'm spoilt for choice,' said Maddie, unsure what to have. There was tea, coffee and a selection of fruit juices and milkshakes. Pasties, sausage rolls, club sandwiches, toasted sandwiches and baked potatoes, all with a good selection of fillings to choose from. Then there was bacon and egg pie, various types of sandwiches made with brown or white bread, not to mention the plethora of pastries and cakes to choose from on display behind the glass fronted counter. Eventually she settled on two. 'Hmm – not sure whether to have the pasty or the club sandwich.'

Jodie had already decided. 'Think I'll try a toasty. Hawaiian looks good – ham, cheese and pineapple.'

'No – think I'll stick to the pasty.' Maddie put the menu back before she could change her mind.

A chubby looking waitress appeared by their table. 'What can I get you girls?' she asked cheerily, the black half apron she wore looking uncomfortably tight around her amble waistline Maddie thought, as she slid her hand into the front concealed pocket and pulled out a notepad.

Without hesitation Jodie said. 'Two coffees

please.'

The waitress took a pencil from behind her ear and started scribbling. 'Anything to eat? I can come back again if you need more time.'

'I'll have the Hawaiian toasty,' Jodie said, looking at Maddie.

'And I'll have a steak pasty please.'

'Okay, that's two coffees, a Hawaiian toasty and a steak pasty,' the waitress read it back. 'Thanks, won't be too long.' She turned and disappeared through a swing door on the far side of the room that they assumed was the entrance to the kitchen.

They planned to reach St Neot around tea time, where they would have something more substantial from the restaurant or fish and chip shop shown in the guide book. If they got hungry along the eight-mile route, they could snack on crisps or a bar of chocolate they'd stuffed into their packs earlier that morning. The Copper trail was an ideal hiking break, with plenty of places at the end of each leg to find something to eat. It wasn't a camping trip; that was completely different, and they would have struggled anyway to carry all the food and cooking gear needed to sustain themselves. Maddie thought her backpack was heavy enough already and she wasn't in training for some sadistic army entrance test. The downside was not being able to get a hot shower or a bath, but at least they had the use of public toilets where they were going.

'Two coffees.' The cheery waitress was back. 'Food won't be long.' She slid a tray into the middle of the table that held two cups, a jug of milk and a bowl of sugar.

'Thanks,' both girls said, as their drinks were placed in front of them.

'You girls going camping?' Hikers were a common sight during the summer months and she couldn't fail to see the backpacks sitting behind them.

'Oh – we're doing the Copper Trail around the moor,' Jodie replied, pulling her cup closer.

The waitress looked surprised. 'Rather you than me. That's some walk. Now, that's got to be – what? Fifty or sixty miles, isn't it?'

'Sixty,' Jodie affirmed.

'We're only doing half of it,' Maddie revealed, smiling. 'Thirty miles is more than enough for me.'

'Thirty miles would be *too* much for me,' the waitress said incredulously. 'Have you been on the moor before?'

Both girls shook their heads. 'Nope,' Jodie said, looking at Maddie. 'I'm afraid to admit, but we're new to all this walking malarkey. It seemed a good idea at the time though.'

'My poor feet might disagree with you by the time we've finished.' Maddie hadn't lost her sense of humour either.

The waitress laughed as she picked up the

empty tray from the table. 'Well, if you don't mind me saying keep to the trail won't you. The weather can change real fast around here. Before you know it a mist can come down and it gets thick because of the high ground and all. I've come out of the café sometimes at the end of my shift and you literally couldn't see the houses opposite – that's how bad it was.'

'Oh, we will,' Jodie said. 'Thanks for the advice anyway.'

'Food won't be long,' she repeated, before turning on her heel and using the tray to clear one of the tables beside them that had just been vacated.

Jodie grinned at Maddie, remembering that film again, the scene in the pub where one of the locals had told the two backpackers something uncannily similar. 'Keep to the trail lads – stay away from the moors,' she said in a spooky voice minus the Yorkshire accent.

This time Jodie's banter failed to illicit a laugh from her friend. The memory had come back to Maddie, like someone flicking on a light switch in her head and making everything as clear as crystal. It had always been there, stored deep in her subconscious along with all the other day to day trivia that the conscious mind didn't need to remember, only rushing to the surface when triggered by something.

Maddie's reflective look hadn't gone unnoticed by Jodie. 'You okay Maddie?'

'Huh...?

'Looks like you've seen a ghost.' Jodie sipped her drink. 'What's up?'

'That's what she said – the woman on the train –' Her voice was barely a whisper.

'What woman?'

Maddie's head was clearing fast now. 'There was an old woman on the train, sat opposite me. She said the same thing, about how the weather can change on the moor... she said a mist can come down before you know it.'

'Oh. everyone knows that, don't they? It's a coincidence that's all,' she said, fluttering her hand dismissively. 'I wouldn't think any more about it.'

'No – not that,' Maddie said firmly. 'It was something else she said when I walked away...'

'What?'

After a brief struggle, the precise words came back to her, and she looked into Jodie's puzzled eyes. 'The old lady said, take care the both of you. Those were her exact words.'

'And?' Jodie pressed her. Although confounded by Maddie's odd behaviour she kept her tone good natured, not wishing to remonstrate with her friend.

Maddie's eyes widened. 'I didn't mention you in the conversation. As far as she was concerned I was

55

on my own – so why would she say that...?'

Jodie went quiet momentarily before shrugging her shoulders. 'I don't know and I wouldn't worry about it to be honest. You must have said something to make her think that. And anyway, what girl in their right mind would go hiking around the moor on their own anyway?'

Maddie fell silent. She held her cup with both hands, elbows on the table and sipped from it thoughtfully. The old woman *had* said that, hadn't she?

'Look, you probably did mention us,' Jodie reassured her. 'And just forgot you had, that's all. You said you were walking away at the time so it's possible you might have misheard what she said. Couldn't you have?'

'Maybe,' Maddie partly agreed, already questioning her memory of the event. She accepted she'd been preoccupied with finding her backpack and getting off the train in time. There was no doubt about that. So...could she have misheard the old lady amongst all the confusion caused by the noise of the train, the stifled music and the children playing in their seats? Could she have...?

Her thoughts were brushed aside when the cheery waitress hovered over them, two plates of food in her hands.

'Pasty?'

'That's me thanks,' Maddie said.

'And a toasty,' the waitress said, placing it in front of Jodie. 'Enjoy your food – and if you need anything else just give me a shout.' She smiled broadly at both girls before disappearing again.

'I'm starving,' Maddie remarked, looking down at the glowing hot pasty. She took her knife and cut through the golden-brown crust, releasing a waft of steam and a meaty potato aroma that assailed her nostrils, making her stomach grumble in anticipation.

Soon, all thoughts of their previous conversation had faded, replaced by the desire to eat and lost amongst discussions about the trip ahead of them. Jodie had her map on the table, folded small into a more manageable size. She had found a place called Golitha Falls, an ancient woodland with babbling brooks running through it and rich in wildlife. It was a popular beauty spot with visitors, especially at this time of the year. Although not on their route it wasn't far from the main trail and might be worth investigating. Maddie had agreed with her, realising it would be another chance to get some great photos and both were keen to take in as many of the sights on offer in the short time they had available to them.

The sheep was in the narrow road, looking at them blankly when they came out of the café.

'Oh, it's you again buddy,' Jodie quipped as she

got her backpack on again. 'The road blocker of Bodmin Moor.'

'How can you tell it's the same one?' Maddie teased. 'They all look the same to me.'

Jodie played along with the joke. 'The red paint there – on its rump,' she pointed.

'Ha ha. They've all got that, haven't they? Maybe he's just reminding you that this is his territory and you're just a visitor.'

'Yeah, maybe,' Jodie smiled, checking her watch. 'Anyway, it's one o'clock now. Ready to make a move?'

'I am now I've had something to eat.'

Before setting off, Jodie looked at her map. 'Golitha Falls is about four miles from here. We should do it in a couple of hours or so.'

It wasn't long before they saw the sign for the Copper Trail nailed to a wooden post just outside the village perimeter. The track was wide enough for them to walk two abreast, a welcome relief to the single file they'd been forced to take to the stone circles earlier.

'So, how do you reckon on doing in two hours?' asked Maddie, matching the bigger girls stride.

'Simple. Average walking speed is about two and a half miles an hour,' the ex-girl scout explained. 'That's without dawdling. If you factor in carrying a back pack that'll slow you down a bit, maybe down two miles an hour, even one mile an hour if it's quite hilly. So, I played safe and went for two.'

'Smart ass,' Maddie smirked. 'Well, at least it's not a race, is it?'

The question was more of a statement and a subtle reminder to Jodie not to get too carried away with her pace. Maddie felt the bigger girl could easily outpace her if she wanted to and she didn't fancy struggling to keep up. After all, it was a walking holiday and not a forced march.

'More like a brisk walk I'd call it,' Jodie cheekily replied. 'You could use a little exercise. Sitting in a classroom all day isn't good for you.'

'Speak for yourself. I'll remind you of that when I graduate and get a nice well paid job in the city on thirty grand a year.'

'Ha ha – you'll be able to afford one of them over priced gym memberships then,' Jodie laughed.

Their light-hearted banter was cut short when they saw a group of dog walkers coming towards them, and Maddie dropped in behind Jodie to allow them past. They greeted each other with 'lovely day, isn't it?' and 'good afternoon,' as they went by each other. They were followed a short time later by a couple of joggers, managing just a quick 'hi' as they ran past, the exertion causing them to pant like dogs in the warm weather.

At one point they came across some disused

mine works and they stopped to take some photos, their chimneys stacks pointing finger like to the sky, relics of a bygone era when the copper mining industry thrived around these parts of the moor and provided a much-needed livelihood to the people that once lived here; hence the name, Copper Moor Trail. It wasn't uncommon to find wild ponies grazing here alongside the sheep and cattle, incongruous though it might have seemed. Buzzards and sometimes peregrines circled relentlessly overhead, looking for their next meal. There were plenty of rodents and large insects to choose from on the moor. Living creatures where not the only inhabitants they soon discovered when they came across the skeletal remains of a small animal – they couldn't decide what it was – its white bones long since picked clean by scavengers no doubt. Scattered bones of something unrecognisable Maddie could deal with. She just hoped she wouldn't come across a recently dead carcass somewhere, swarming with flies and infested with maggots. The very thought of it turned her stomach.

An hour later, Maddie was feeling exhilarated, the combination of fresh air, exercise and sunshine serving to lighten her mood. The pack felt comfortable on her back, nothing chafed or dug into her sides and even the new boots she had failed to break in properly felt comfortable on her feet.

'That's it, I can't wait any longer,' Jodie said, pulling up. 'Need a pee.' She looked about for somewhere suitable to go and was relieved to see that no one else was around just now. A few trees would have been a welcome sight though, she thought.

Maddie felt she could go too. 'How about over there?' She pointed out some thick gorse bushes a stone's throw away.

'That'll do fine,' Jodie said hurrying towards it.

'I'll keep an eye out.' Maddie almost had to jog to keep up. 'Then I need to go too.'

Jodie dumped her backpack and disappeared behind the thicket while Maddie stood watch.

'Watch out for the prickles!' she hollered.

Jodie had squatted out of sight. 'Ha ha.'

Maddie could hear her peeing but waited until she had finished before speaking. 'I'd hurry up if I was you. There's someone coming.'

'Shit!' A mad scramble of jeans pulling up, belt buckle jangling, made Maddie chuckle.

Jodie stuck her head up. 'Bitch!' Fell for that one, didn't she?

Maddie went next and as Jodie was getting her pack on again she wondered if Maddie would fall for a similar prank. Unlikely, she decided. But just then an opportunity presented itself causing her to grin. 'I see you've got an admirer Maddie.'

'Eh?' She had just finished and yanked up her knickers. Peering over the bush, jeans around her ankles, she followed Jodie's gaze to a spot just left of her.

'We've got a peeping tom.'

Maddie couldn't help but laugh at the rabbit sitting there, eyeing her curiously, its nose twitching. 'Go on – scoot,' she said, waving it away with the back of her hand. 'Get out of here thumper!' The rabbit refused to budge which heightened the already delighted look on Jodie's face that she'd managed to get her own back.

It wasn't long after setting off again when they saw two figures in the far distance, and if snow had covered the moor just then, they might well have mistaken them for cross country skiers as they drove their trekking poles into the ground in front of them. They thought they might meet them head on further along the track, but realised they weren't on the same route when they angled off sharply, disappearing across the moors barren landscape.

Before you know it, a mist can come down in no time. Now, Maddie thought, as she walked in the bright warm July sunshine, visibility clear for miles around with that deep blue sky overhead, how overstated the old lady's ominous warning now seemed.

FOUR

They reached the village of St Neot earlier than
expected, partly because they'd made good time
across the level terrain but mainly because they'd
decided not to visit Golitha Falls which was further
from the main trail than they'd originally thought.
They wanted to get to the village around four
o'clock, find somewhere suitable to pitch their tent,
before getting something to eat and maybe a drink
or two in the pub later before settling down for the
night.

St Neot was a stark contrast to the quiet hamlet
they'd left behind. The sound of a brass band
mixed with hoots of laughter greeted them as they
entered the busy narrow street, bright coloured
bunting hanging above them between the houses
either side; little flags poked out from windows, or

carried in the hands of excited children with brightly painted animal faces. 'SUMMER FESTIVAL' the banner overhead proclaimed, and it looked like the whole village was out to celebrate it Maddie thought, as well as some delighted tourists who stood around taking pictures with their cameras or on their phones.

What a stroke of luck, the girls thought, as they fell in behind the small crowd of people gathered in front of them, the brass band growing louder the further down the street they went. Soon, they came to the village square where the musicians were playing from a bandstand and the bulk of the crowd had now gathered. Wandering amongst the crowd were Morris dancers and people in fancy dress: swash buckling pirates, colourful court jesters and others dressed in period costume. Overexcited kids munched on pink candy floss and toffee apples and licked oversized lollipops that seemed to last forever, as they strolled hand in hand with mum or dad.

The girls joined a small queue that had formed beside a burger van, drawn there by the enticing smell of fried onions, hot dogs and burgers that wafted through the air. They both ordered jumbo sized hot dogs with onions, Maddie smothering hers in ketchup, before eating them greedily as they stood there taking in the festivities all around them. Their hunger subdued, they grabbed two coffees before wandering off through the crowd of revellers again, curious to discover what else was happening in the village.

They came across a group who were gathered around a horse and carriage that was on display on a grassy area behind the bandstand, its driver sitting atop in Victorian style dress complete with cloak and tricorne hat, an ominous looking black whip in his hand. The girls decided it would make a great photo and they squeezed their way through the crowd that seemed to be getting larger by the minute and threatening to overspill the village square.

It was a magnificent horse Maddie thought, its jet black shiny coat matching the colour of the smart unfussy open top carriage standing behind it. A man, also attired in Victorian clothes, was holding the bridle as a young girl reached up nervously to touch the horses head, her mother hovering over her and giving her little words of encouragement.

'It won't hurt you,' she said softly, watching her daughters hand jerking back tentatively. The woman stroked it herself. 'See – it's okay, isn't it?'

Realising it wouldn't bite, the girl managed to touch it, patting its nose rather than stroking the length of its head, wary of lingering too long.

'There see – told you it would be alright, didn't I?'

The little girl looked very pleased with herself and she peered up expectantly to her mother. 'Can I have an ice cream now mummy? You promised!'

The woman smiled down at her daughter. 'Of course you can pumpkin,' she said, taking her hand and leading her away, the little girl chittering excitedly about her impending treat until her shrill voice became lost amongst the cacophony of the crowd.

The man by the horse smiled as they approached, and gave Maddie an approving nod before she stepped close and ran her hand along the animal's thickly muscled neck. Maddie could almost sense the wild power of the animal as she stroked the length of its head, before leaning around to peer inside the blinker that obstructed its vision. The bulbous staring eye that saw her lolled about, its ears twitching and Maddie pulled back quickly hoping she hadn't startled the beast but it remained perfectly still. It was obviously comfortable around people, she thought.

'Take a picture Jodie,' Maddie said, turning to face her now. 'Try and get the carriage in too if you can.'

Jodie backed up, holding the phone up in front of her, then turning it sideways to get everything in frame. 'Okay – ready? Big smile.'

Maddie cheekily asked the man holding the bridle if it would be okay if she could sit up top with the driver and have her photo taken. 'Yes, don't see why not,' he happily agreed.

She started climbing up and the driver swivelled in his seat. 'Come on up missy,' he said, proffering his hand. His skin looked unusually white, contrasting starkly with his dark piercing eyes and the thick black hair that protruded from his hat that made him appear scarecrow like, and if Maddie hadn't known any better she might have thought he was an albino. *But didn't they have white hair and pink eyes?* She wasn't sure. There was little warmth to his hands when they clasped and she thought his slender bony fingers seemed feminine for a man.

Jodie moved around to the front and took a couple of head on snaps. Then they swapped places and Maddie took one of her.

Later in the day, they had fish and chips in 'Betty's Fish n' Chip' shop followed by ice cream and coffee. It was there that the owner told them about a small field at the opposite end of the village open to use by hikers wanting to pitch a tent for the night. Provided it was for one night and they left the area spotless when they left they were quite welcome to use it for free. It was owned by a local farmer, who provided the village pub and shops with produce from his farm, demand rising during the summer months when the tourists arrived in droves. The more visitors spending money in the village the better, and it didn't hurt to offer his field out for free as a way of appeasing them. Apparently, he didn't have much use for that field anyway as his livestock had outgrown it several years since.

After eating, they wasted no time in heading out of the village in search of the field, finding it immediately when they looked over the gate and saw another tent was already pitched there. They erected theirs without much difficulty, unrolled their bed rolls and sleeping bags, stowed the packs inside and returned to the village for a quick drink before settling down for their first night in the open.

The Coach and Horses pub looked just about the same as every other village ale house. It had that cottage style look with baskets of bright flowers hanging over the entrance and wooden picnic benches out front with umbrellas shading the tables.

They peered up at the colourful sign over the doorway. The coach driver was bent forward, an expression of urgency on his face as he whipped the startled horses into a frenzy in front, a bewildered portly looking gentleman peering out the window and clutching his hat that threatened to fly off at any minute.

Jodie spoke first. 'At least it's not called the Slaughtered Lamb.'

'I'd give it a miss if it was.' Maddie recalled that was the name of the pub in the movie and for a moment she half expected the whole pub to go silent, the locals turning and staring at them when they went inside, just like what had happened to the two lads when they'd entered the pub and asked innocently what that symbol was inscribed above the dart board.

As they entered the busy pub – which was a mixture of tourists and locals – no one paid any attention to them as they headed for the bar. The room didn't fall silent, nobody turned to stare at them, and more importantly Maddie noticed, there was no five-pointed star inscribed on the wall above the dart board either.

They took their drinks and headed back outside into the warm late afternoon sunshine, Jodie grabbing a table when she saw the people sitting there getting up to leave.

Maddie sipped the cold shandy she had ordered, then picked up her phone and thumbed through the photo gallery. 'Got some great pics today. They've come out really well.'

Jodie was reviewing hers. 'Me too – surprised half of them have come out like they have. It was only a cheap phone.'

'As long as it does the job, eh?'

'I daren't get a new one though. I've given mum and dad enough hints recently and I have a funny feeling the one I'm after might appear on my birthday.'

'You hope,' Maddie teased, remembering Jodie's birthday was a couple of months away.

'Oh, I will. Mum put me off last week when I nearly bought one in town, so if that's not a dead giveaway they're getting me it I don't know what is.'

'Jammy git,' Maddie said. 'Well – the only photo missing from here is the Beast of Bodmin. I promised mum I'd text her a copy when I saw it.'

'Did you? That's if you live to tell the tale, you mean,' Jodie half-joked.

Maddie finished looking at the photos and placed the phone down on the table. 'Do you think there is such a thing?' she asked. 'The beast of Bodmin Moor?' She took a longer sip of her drink this time as she waited for a response.

Jodie appeared thoughtful. 'I know we've had newspaper and eye witness reports, but you know how the media likes to exaggerates that sort of thing, don't they? I'm not sure what to think to be honest. But I don't believe it's some sort of supernatural beast either the way its portrayed in books or the movies, like something from the hound of the Baskervilles.'

'No, that's stretching things a bit too far. You don't think it could be a big cat then?'

'That's what the zoologists reckon anyway as

the most likely explanation, and I'm inclined to agree with them. But even if it were true you'd be lucky to get close enough. It wouldn't hang around while you took a photo.'

'Weren't they released into the wild years ago when the laws changed about keeping exotic pets at home? I remember reading that.'

Jodie had heard that too. It had been fashionable in wealthy circles to keep exotic animals in home zoos until it had been banned by the government in the 1970's. Giant snakes, reptiles and big cats such as lions, tigers and pumas being the most popular, apparently.

'I suppose it's possible Maddie. There's plenty of wildlife out there to sustain them, not to mention the rabbits and rodents around farmland. If anyone knows that I should,' the farm girl stressed, raising her glass to her lips and taking a long sip of the cool lemonade she had ordered.

'Well, as long as it stays away from our tent tonight I couldn't care less.'

'Oh, I don't think you have anything to worry about there miss.' They weren't expecting the disembodied voice and it took them aback.

Looking across to the table beside them they saw a middle-aged man, well-tanned, wearing jeans and checked shirt with sleeves rolled up sitting with a pint in front of him. That he worked outdoors was immediately apparent by his craggy and weather beaten features, and if this had been near the coast Maddie reasoned he might perhaps have been a fisherman.

'Apologies for interrupting,' he grinned inanely. 'But I couldn't help hearing what you were saying about the Bodmin Beast.'

'That's okay,' Maddie said.

They could tell by his accent he was Cornish.

'Do you live local then?' asked Jodie, leaning forward to peer around Maddie who partly blocked her view. Maddie sat back.

The man leaned forward, folding his arms on the table. 'Certainly do miss. I've lived on the moor all my life, so I have. Most of my family came from around here. There's a farm a mile down the road from here. I help out there most days.'

'Do you believe in the beast then?' Maddie sensed he had something to impart. Why else would he interrupt them?

He pondered the question before answering. 'Well – believing is one thing and seeing is another, isn't it? But – sad to say though, I haven't seen it, no, not in all the years I've lived here.'

'Oh!' Maddie said. She'd half expected to hear some tale from this local farm hand who'd spent his whole life living and working on the moor, and on how he'd not only seen the beast himself, but perhaps stumbled across it up close and had managed to escape with his life and lived to tell the tale. But she wasn't going to hear any of that.

He took a swig of beer and kept hold of his glass. 'But I have seen evidence of it.'

Finally, Maddie thought. 'Go on,' she prompted him.

Both girls were curious now, his friendly manner quelling the natural wariness they felt from the stranger who had introduced himself. He seemed harmless enough.

'Well – it was four years ago,' he began. 'Never forget it. It was a bloody hard winter that year, bitterly cold and we had snow solid for two months straight. I don't think anyone around here can remember a winter as bad as that one. I remember Bill saying we better take the tractor – he's the farmer I work for. Anyhow – the snow was that deep you couldn't risk taking the land rover out to the fields, that's how bad it was and the rover's a four-wheel drive.'

He took another gulp of ale, putting the half empty glass down this time and wiping his lips with the back of his hand. The first and second finger were tobacco stained Maddie saw.

'Anyway, we had to mend this fence way across the other side of the field, so I jumped down off the tractor and opened the gate so Bill could drive the tractor through. I shut the gate and was about to get back on the tractor again when Bill started shouting something and pointing from the cab. It was then that I saw it – the tracks in the snow.'

'Really?' exclaimed Maddie.

Jodie was more than familiar with animal tracks on the farm. 'I take it they weren't fox or badger marks then?'

He shook his head. 'Oh, no miss. These were bigger, much bigger.' He held up his hand and showed the gap between his first finger and thumb. His eyes widened, comically. 'They must have been four inches long.'

'A large dog maybe?' Maddie suggested, yet secretly hoping it wasn't.

'Nope, wasn't a dog miss. A dog leaves claw marks when it walks. Now a cat, that's different. They can retract their claws and don't normally leave marks except maybe if they're running or if they make a sudden change in direction. But that's about the only time you might see them. No, it was a cat alright – a big one though.'

Jodie nodded in agreement. 'That's true,' she said looking at Maddie. 'I've seen loads of dog and fox tracks around the farm and cats too come to that. You can spot the difference if you know what you're looking for.'

'Anyway,' he continued, 'I wouldn't worry too much about one bothering you, if there was a big cat I mean. They like to stay well away from humans, and there's plenty of food out there when they want it.' The words he spoke next were directed at Maddie. 'As for getting a photo miss,' he said, shaking his head. 'Not a chance in hell. But I'd be the first to congratulate you if you did,' he chortled. Sensing he might have overstepped the mark, he added: 'No offence mind.'

'None taken,' Maddie said.

'But your friends quite right,' he said, turning his gaze to the bigger girl. 'When she said there's plenty of wildlife out there. A big cat would take a fox no problem. Then there's livestock. Plenty of sheep have been found mauled and half eaten on farmland or on the moors over the years.' He drained the last dregs from his glass and gave a small sigh of satisfaction.

'But wouldn't we hear more reports about it if farm animals were being attacked?' Maddie asked. 'It would be all over the news, wouldn't it?'

'Not necessarily, no. Especially in the more remote parts of the country. Some of these farms are in the middle of nowhere and folk tend to keep to themselves. Anyway, half the time it's a fox that's responsible and even wild dogs have been known to attack sheep.'

Jodie glanced at Maddie. 'True enough. They'd be reluctant to report anything unless they were sure it was something out the ordinary. Even then they'd probably want to deal with it themselves and keep it in the family, organise a local hunt or something and attempt to track the animal down.

The last thing they'd want is a load of reporters or a television crew getting in their way, not to mention the anti-hunt protestors and animal rights activists who'd be all over them like a rash.'

'I see,' Maddie said, wondering to herself now what the true scale of unexplained animal attacks might be due to either complacency or a lack of unequivocal evidence.

'But reports have made the news over the years,' the farm hand said. 'We tend to forget them, that's all. Like that lorry driver who said a lion had jumped out right in front of him as he was passing a claypit. Somewhere out St Austell way if I remember rightly.'

'A lion?' Maddie said disbelievingly.

'I remember that,' Jodie said. 'It was on the West Country News. The police investigated and found white paw prints crossing the road...'

'Did they?' Maddie asked.

The farm hand nodded. 'Yep, that's right. But they said there was nothing to worry about and it posed no danger to the public. Bloody idiots!'

The girls laughed.

'And there was that woman in St Austell too,' he carried on. 'Said she saw a cat up a tree but it was three times the size of her dog. The branch it was sitting on caught her attention when she saw it bobbing up and down. Anyway, she said she couldn't see the head; just the body and tail of the animal.' He rose from his seat, leaving the empty glass on the table. 'Don't get too excited though. Turns out the sightings occurred around the same time a lynx was on the loose from a zoo in Dartmoor.'

'Did they capture it?' Maddie asked.

'Luckily, yes. After it had been on the run for nearly three weeks though. Tranquilized it, so they did. It was a big embarrassment to the zoo, and if you ask me they were bloody lucky nobody was killed. The sightings stopped soon after.'

'Ah, that could explain it then,' said Maddie, sounding slightly disappointed.

'That one it might,' Jodie conceded. 'But it doesn't explain all of them. There've been reports up and down the country and as far away as Scotland...'

'Well,' the farm hand said, glancing at his watch now. 'I'd love to sit here chatting all afternoon and all but I better not keep the missus waiting – she'll have my tea on the table soon and I'll be in all sorts of trouble if I don't...' He broke off with a laugh. 'Anyway – nice to meet the both of you.'

'You too,' both girls said simultaneously.

Before leaving he looked at Maddie. 'Hope you get your photo miss. Good day to you both.'

They watched him hurry away, disappearing amongst the locals and tourists milling about in the narrow busy street.

Jodie took their empty glasses and returned to the pub for a refill, leaving Maddie to mull over their conversation with the farm hand. He'd given her plenty to think about, the idea intriguing her more than ever now that the Bodmin Beast could be very real and roaming the moor as they sat here enjoying a cool drink in the late afternoon sunshine. How ironic that would be, she thought. But what were the chances of *them* encountering it in only three days, when someone who had spent his whole life out here had seen nothing but some footprints in the snow that would have disappeared in the subsequent thaw leaving no evidence whatsoever. But it was human nature to think that way, wasn't it? You could be the lucky one. Like the curious visitors drawn to Loch Ness in Scotland every year, hoping *they* might be the ones to catch a glimpse of the elusive monster in the lake and perhaps even photograph or capture it on film. A tall order, perhaps? Never mind the locals who had lived there for years and seen nothing at all. But stranger things had happened, Maddie thought. There was always a chance. And when you least expected it.

It was still light when they decided to return to the tent. They'd need a good night's sleep before the next leg of their hike, and although her feet felt okay Maddie would be glad to get her boots and socks off and give her feet a good massage. They might not be in such good shape tomorrow afternoon after walking the thirteen miles to Bodmin, she thought. She'd never walked that far before, especially with a pack on her back.

They crawled inside the cramped space and sat on their sleeping bags, both girls wasting no time in getting their boots and socks off and giving their feet a welcome rub. Maddie stripped down to her bra and knickers and placed her folded jeans and tee shirt on top of her boots which he placed strategically at the bottom of her sleeping bag. She was glad now she'd used the pub loo before leaving as she didn't fancy scrabbling around in the middle of the night if she needed to get out for a pee. But at least she knew where her boots and clothes were, although it would be a bit of a hassle. Not that she was worried either that someone might see her. There was only one other tent, pitched across the far side of the field and it would be dark later anyway, and in the absence of any street lamps she realised she could probably run around stark naked in the field and nobody would be any the wiser. The thought made Maddie laugh to herself.

Despite the pitch blackness of the tent, the girls faced each other as they lay on their sides, tucked up snugly in their sleeping bags. Maddie was surprised at just how quiet it was, the silence only interrupted by the occasional car driving past on the narrow road behind them, eventually falling silent as the village succumbed to the darkness and the locals settled down for the night. And it made her wonder if the people living here appreciated just how fortunate they were not having to listen to the incessant night sounds of the city: an aeroplane soaring overhead, a train thundering by perhaps only feet away from a back garden or the muffled sounds of city traffic intruding through a half open window.

It was so quiet in fact that Maddie felt her ears buzzing and thought if a pin dropped beside her now she would probably hear it. Later, when darkness prevailed she lay there listening to the sound of a fox screaming in the distance and a sheep bleating from a nearby field.

'It's a fox,' Jodie sniggered when Maddie asked what that screaming noise was.

'Christ! is that what they sound like? I've never heard one before.'

'Are you kidding?'

'Nope. I bet you've seen a few of them around the farm though, haven't you?'

'A couple of times, yes. They soon scarpered though when the dog saw them and started barking like mad.'

'Well,' Maddie admitted. 'When I heard that eerie cry I thought it was a wolf or something. Don't know why I thought that though.' Just then, an image formed in her mind of a wolf howling at the moon.

'There's no wolves in England, not anymore. Maybe a werewolf though,' Jodie whispered. 'It's the wolfman Maddie – he's coming to get us. Or maybe it's the Beast of Bodmin Moor...'

'Shit Jodie! don't even joke about it.' Her half serious tone descended into nervous laughter when her friend started giggling.

'Seriously though Jodie, that was scary. If I'd been on the moor in the dark and heard that it would have frightened me half to death.' It was her turn to laugh this time and in the darkness of the tent she couldn't see Jodie's poker faced expression.

'What?'

Maddie tried to stifle her giggle. 'I thought – the fox I mean. I thought – they barked, like a dog.'

'A dog? Ha ha ha – very funny. Want to hear something scary?'

'Like what?'

'If you've heard it before just tell me, okay?'

'Get on with it,' said Maddie. 'But after listening to that fox screaming like that I don't think you'll better it.'

'A couple were driving through a forest one night,' Jodie began. 'When their car ran out of petrol. They see lights from a house in the distance. The boyfriend gets out of the car and tells his girlfriend to lock all the doors while he goes to get help. Time passes and her boyfriend hasn't come back. Not long after, she hears banging on the roof of the car, then the sound of sirens as police cars appear out of now where, their blue lights flashing...'

'Yes – go one.' Maddie was intrigued but wasn't sure she wanted to hear the punch line.

'Anyway. A policeman shouts out to her, telling her to get slowly out of the car and walk towards him but under no circumstances was she to look back. She got out the car, real slow, like the policeman told her and walked over to him but she couldn't resist the urge to look back...' Her pause was deliberate.

'Yeess?' Maddie's voice wavered.

'On top of the car she saw a man with a bloodied axe in one hand and her boyfriend's head in the other which he was banging on the roof of the car. He was some lunatic who'd escaped from an asylum earlier that day. Luckily they'd just caught up with him.'

'Shit Jodie! That's not true, is it?'

'No – don't think so,' Jodie giggled nervously. 'Creepy though, isn't it. I read it on the internet. But who knows, eh? There's plenty of psychos about.'

'Well, that's enough of that. I won't get to sleep now.' She wriggled deeper into her sleeping bag, shrugging the thought from her mind before it could dwell too long on the grisly tale Jodie had just told her. But she knew it would only be temporary and it would come back to haunt her when she least expected it. When she was trying to get off to sleep. Like the umpteen times she'd watched those horror films on late night tv and retired to bed telling herself under the darkness of the covers that it was only make believe. It wasn't real. They were just actors after all, weren't they? It had never worked though.

She lay there for what seemed a very long time, her mind tuning in to every night sound around her, feeling very vulnerable in a tent in the middle of nowhere, and it suddenly occurred to her the only thing protecting her from the outside world was a flimsy waterproof piece of fabric with a zip down the front. And her mind started playing tricks on her. *There weren't any of those asylums around here. Were there? And what about the Beast of Bodmin...?*

An owl hooted, and that fox was screaming again. It still sounded like a wolf Maddie thought. Eventually though, and not as late as she thought it was, tiredness overcame her and she drifted towards sleep unaware it was even happening.

FIVE

He'd been sitting there in the pub when they'd walked in. Ben always sat in the corner out the way, his red base-ball cap pulled down perhaps a little lower than it needed to be. Not that he was being furtive or anything; he just liked to keep to himself, that's all, away from prying eyes and it wouldn't pay to draw any attention to himself.

Every Friday afternoon he'd sit there waiting for the right opportunity to present itself, and there'd been a few of them over the past three weeks but they were either in girly groups because it made them feel safe or bloody courting couples and never on their own. But what woman in her right mind would be out here on her own in the middle of the moor? Now tonight was different. He didn't often see two of them, unless they were part of a larger group waiting outside. But he could always check later.

The brunette looked okay, a big strapping girl he'd noticed with even bigger breasts and wide hips, those thunderous thighs looking like they could clamp right around a man and squeeze the life out of him like a boa constrictor. But no – she could be difficult. The bitch looked strong and appeared to match his five-foot eight frame and she had a purposeful look about her. No – she could give him trouble. Anyway, she was a bit too butch, Ben thought.

Now, blondie over there – well, she was a different kettle of fish altogether. After dismissing the butch looking one he thought all his Christmases had come at once now. She wouldn't give him any problems at all with that lithe smaller frame, the pert little nose and small yet firm breasts jutting from her tee shirt. She wasn't over curvaceous like her mate but everything was in the right place and the most important thing was that he'd fancied her as soon as he'd laid eyes on her. He wondered if they were lesbians, not that it bothered him but the very idea filled him with a strange sense of perverted satisfaction. That's if they were on their own of course. Perhaps their *boyfriends were waiting outside? But then, why would they be?*

Ben felt like some big game hunter, sitting there and taking everything in, stalking his prey and waiting, just waiting for the right one to come along. And it had, it seemed, if his hunch was right and they were definitely alone. The backpacks they carried had given the game away, like all the others that had passed through here since the beginning of the summer. Like they did every summer.

He'd watched them as they waited to get served at the crowded bar, careful to avoid making direct eye contact with either of them. His baseball cap was a godsend in that department, not to mention the crowd that had gathered here to celebrate the village summer festival.

When he saw them go outside, taking their drinks with them, he'd already made his mind up. It was now or never. Take one step at a time Benny, he thought, scolding himself for allowing that term of endearment to dare enter his mind again. She'd called him that. Benny. His mother always had, and he hated it. So, it was all her fault when it got out what his little pet name was and everyone started calling him it, including the kids he went to school with. She might as well have stuck a label on his back.

Getting back on track, and taking one step at a time, he realised it wouldn't do any harm just to follow them outside – take a little look – make sure they were on their own. Nobody would notice him amongst the festival crowd. And the waiting had paid off now, hadn't it? The perfect opportunity had come his way at last.

Ben had to hover around outside for a bit, waiting until a seat became available. But it didn't matter. The street was packed with people, tourists and locals alike, and nobody took any notice of him as he stood there with a pint in his hand, leaning casually against the wall at the front of the pub just right of the entrance. He blended in nicely and no one could suspect a thing. And anyway, he wasn't doing anything wrong.

They wouldn't notice him either but he could see them. Unless they got up from their table and headed back into the pub and then they'd have to go right past him of course. But he'd have plenty of warning and could just move out the way. They were sitting a couple of feet in front of him with their backs to him, chatting with Pete the bloody farm hand. What a prat! He'd recognised him straight away by the bald patch on the back of his head he was

*now forced to look at and the shoddy clothes
he normally wore. Married to that fat old cow –
wasn't he – he didn't know her name? Now,
here he was, bold as brass, keeping them
company, chatting them up by the looks of it
too, giving them his bullshit stories about the
Beast of Bodmin Moor and all that, reeling
them in and telling the girlies what they
wanted to hear. Crafty old git. He'd like to see
the look on his face if his missus came along
right now and caught him red handed
nattering with two young women who were
young enough to be his daughters. She'd give
him a right earful.*

*Ben pulled a tobacco pouch from the back
of his jeans and started to roll up a ciggie, all
the time listening in on the conversation just in
front of him. Well – he'd taken the first step,
hadn't he, and he wasn't feeling anywhere
near as nervous as he thought he would. It
was a piece of cake, so far anyway. One step
at a time Benny, the voice in his head
reminded him, and he growled inwardly
against it wishing he could just grab that little
bugger and squeeze the life out of it. It was all
her fault, wasn't it? This damn thing in his
head! You need to get a grip of yourself or
you'll give the game away the normal part of
his mind interrupted, and he quickly calmed*

himself focusing once more on the task in hand.

It was a good job he had too, for Pete was standing up now, without his empty glass. Was he going home now? Ben looked at his watch. He normally did around this time, didn't he? Or would he be tempted to hang around a bit longer because they were here, like a dog sniffing at its dinner. Better get ready in case he picked his glass up – the last thing he needed was him noticing him by the door and stopping for a chat. That wouldn't do, would it? The girls might look his way, and he didn't want that to happen. Not that he was being paranoid or anything; he was being careful that's all. The few people that noticed him the better. That way he couldn't be linked to anything that might happen later. But wasn't he getting ahead of himself a bit? He was only on step one for god's sake, hadn't done nothing wrong, but he could just imagine it though:

'Ben was hanging around the tables where the girls were sat. Yes, of course I'm sure. He was stood near the door when I bumped in to him. We had a little chat in fact. You might want to have a word with him too, eliminate him from your enquiries'.

Ben smirked to himself. Tut tut. They'd be

knocking on his door in no time and he didn't want any of that.

He watched, ready to slink aside if he had to. But he thought there'd be no need, judging by the farm hands body language.

Nope – he's saying goodbye to them, and thank god for small mercies, he told himself, drawing hard on the ciggie between his nicotine stained fingers. He blew out a cloud of blue swirling smoke, making sure to turn his head so it didn't go in their direction. Even that might draw attention, especially from a non-smoker. He'd noticed that before when he'd been out and about in town; the disgusted look some people had given him as he'd stood outside a shop having a smoke and they'd caught a whiff of it as they passed. Supposed to be a free country, wasn't it? Sanctimonious shits – the lot of them, that's what they were.

So, just to get his own back he'd do it on purpose sometimes, standing there and waiting for some unsuspecting victim to come along and then he'd just blow a great big cloud of smoke out just as they were walking past, sniggering to himself when he saw the expression on their face. He was careful though, avoiding anyone bigger than him who looked like they might give him some trouble. The old people were the best, and if it looked like one of them was about to say anything he'd stare right at them as if to say, 'Come on then old man? Want to make something of it, do you?' They never did though, especially if their old dears were with them: 'Come along George. We don't want any trouble. What a horrible man!'

Ben thought about taking the seat now vacant in front of him, but decided against it. One of them might glance his way or even worse, they might strike up a conversation with him – unlikely that it was – perhaps recognising him as a local and wanting information or directions to somewhere or other. Now, wouldn't that be a turn up for the books he chuckled. That would be bloody hilarious. But the more likely scenario was that somebody might remember him having seen him sitting there next to them in his red base-ball cap pulled down just enough so it shaded his eyes from view yet not so much that he couldn't see what was happening around him. He really should do something about that – red wasn't a very inconspicuous colour, was it? Black would have been better.

He watched them finish their drinks, his eyes undressing blondie as her back arched over that tight little waist as she tilted her head back to drain the last of her drink from the glass. She was a slender little thing he thought, and he loved the cute ponytail. He could tug on that.

When he saw butch get up and grab their empty glasses he looked down into his pint, angling his body away from her as she walked right past him into the pub. Phew! Close one that. But it was okay, she hadn't seen his face. She probably hadn't even noticed him anyway with everybody else milling around out here and the constant flow of customers coming in and out all the time. The street was packed, and a good job too.

He waited until butch came out and sat down again next to her mate. He'd looked out the corner of his eye as she'd passed, noting she was about the same height as him – perhaps a tad taller but not much – and he knew taking on both of them was out of the question. The big girl could be a real pain in the ass and he didn't want to risk it. No – with a bit of luck he'd catch blondie on her own – no witnesses and no butch either to have to deal with.

Realising they wouldn't be going anywhere yet because their glasses were still full, Ben nipped back into the pub to get another pint, feeling real good about himself now that step one was coming along nicely, thank you very much. The nervousness had all but gone now, replaced by a growing sense of anticipation and he felt like that big game hunter again as he waited for his prey to walk right into his trap.

A short while later, when he started tailing them through the now not so busy street, being careful to keep his distance, he guessed he'd just successfully started on step number two. Watching was one thing but stalking was a different ball game. One little mistake though and he could be in real trouble if he spooked them and got reported for acting suspiciously. Stalking was a criminal offence now, wasn't it? He'd seen enough of it on the news. Celebrity stalkers they called them. Except butch and blondie weren't celebrities, were they? Anyway, he'd upped the ante now and there was no going back even if he wanted to, the compulsion so strong now to find out where the girls were staying the night. Had to be somewhere close – maybe the field at the end of the village, that's if they'd been tipped off about it though. He'd walked past that field daily on his way to the village, seen the odd tent there now and again and imagined what it'd be like – if only he'd had the nerve – to hide in the hedgerow and just watch for a while.

Until now, that is. And boy didn't he feel great just then, the rising excitement he felt making his heart beat like a drum when he saw them push open the gate and enter the field. Trouble was, he couldn't hang around here until it got dark. That would be asking for trouble. But at least they weren't going anywhere for the time being, and he knew exactly where to find them when he came back later. Provided he could hold his nerve.

He headed back to the village, deciding not to take the opposite direction to the little cottage he lived in just on the outskirts. If he went home now, he might doze off in his armchair like he'd done a hundred times before after spending the afternoon drinking. No – that wouldn't do. It would ruin everything. He'd waited long enough and he might not get this chance again. Maybe not for a long time. He wasn't about to blow it.

It was only a couple of hours later, and he did come back. He'd spent the time back in the pub having a few more drinks and planning in his head the best place to position himself so he could get as close as possible without alerting them to his presence. But then, what was he worrying about? It should be pitch black in that field, provided the moon wasn't *up, and he could stand where he liked. No one would see him. Just the thought of standing there, right outside their tent, knowing they were probably in there half naked as they got undressed for bed, sent a shiver of sexual excitement rippling through his loins and he could feel himself stirring down there already. Christ! What if they were lesbians after all? He might even catch them at it...listening to them doing it only feet away from his trembling hand. Of course, he wouldn't be able to see them, but his imagination would do the rest, wouldn't it?*

A fox screamed in the night but Ben barely registered it as he half-staggered towards the gate, regretting now that he'd had those extra pints of lager. He'd felt okay in the pub. But that was the trouble with the booze, wasn't it? One minute you felt fine, then once outside in the night air – bang – it could come back and bite you on the ass like an angry dog. He'd have to be extra careful now and keep his wits about him.

He put his hands on the gate and steadied himself and he thought he heard stifled laughter coming from inside the field. What the hell were they doing in there? Cracking jokes? He sniggered. Yeah – he knew what they were doing alright, he knew exactly what two giggling girls like that were doing in a tent in the middle of a field, his imagination arousing his senses despite the numbing effects of the drink. No wonder they were on their own out here.

Bracing himself, he took a single deep breath as if it would help clear the fog from his brain, and gently, quietly, pushed the gate open.

It was pitch-dark, despite the million pin pricks of light twinkling through the blackness above him that stretched all the way to the horizon. Good job too, he found himself thinking.

He stood inside the field for a moment and listened, his heart pounding so loud now in his ears that he thought they might even hear it and start screaming their bloody heads off or something. Then he felt a tiny bit anxious at the gravity of what he was doing, pondering the consequences of his actions should he get caught red handed. But it didn't last long. He'd got to step two and the compulsion he now felt was so overwhelming that it had to be satiated. Of course, he could always plead ignorance if it all went wrong. He laughed to himself at the sudden realisation. Maybe being drunk as a skunk wasn't such a bad thing after all. It could even work in his favour and he could play on it, couldn't he? The local Community Support Officer was a jumped-up prat with a chip on his shoulder and could easily be fooled. They weren't real coppers anyway, were they? More like social workers in uniform, he thought. He'd probably be taken home to sleep it off after realising he'd had too much to drink and had simply wandered into the field by accident on his way home from the pub. Getting lost whilst under the influence wasn't a crime.

His footsteps were measured as he moved closer, guided towards the tent by the girly chatting and giggling that reached his ears. A couple of times he had to stop abruptly, aware that his balance was all over the place as he staggered sideways. After taking a deep breath and steadying himself once more, he moved forward again.

Ben stopped a few feet from the tent. That was far enough. But why weren't they laughing now? One of them was talking. It sounded like she was telling a story or something and it took him a few seconds to realise it was the bigger girl that was doing all the yapping, her voice recognisable from earlier when he'd listened to them outside the pub. He thought he might have gotten lucky and perhaps seen the shadows of their naked forms cast by torchlight inside their tent but he could see nothing but darkness. And he found himself wondering what they were wearing in there, especially blondie. Or perhaps she liked to sleep nude? God! They might even be sharing the same bloody sleeping bag! He'd love to find out – but that would have to wait for another time, wouldn't it?

Ben swayed a bit and had to catch himself and for one awful minute he thought he might hiccup and he clasped a hand over his mouth just in case. It was just a burp. He could hear Blondie talking now, reassuring him his little slip-up had gone unnoticed.

He stood there for a few seconds, swaying from side to side, and when he realised nothing much was happening down there he began to feel frustrated and a little taken aback at his own inadequacy.

Come on Benny! That tormenting voice was back again, right inside his head. What's wrong with you? You plucked up the courage to go through with it and now you're just standing there like a complete idiot. You got some sort of problem? the voiced continued to mock. You ought to see a doctor about that you know. Ha ha ha.

Ben sneered. I've had too much to drink, that's all. If I was sober I'd damn well show you – so why don't you bugger off someplace else. And stop calling me that...

Tut tut. There's no need to get tetchy. You should be used to it by now. They used to call you that at school, didn't they...?

The annoying voice was right, Ben had to admit. It had started at primary school. Oh, it had seemed innocent enough at first, they were six years old at the time and didn't know any better and he hadn't been old enough to take any real offence. It had all seemed just a bit of light hearted fun, hadn't it? Until he'd moved up to secondary school at the ripe old age of eleven...

Benny's not a man. No wonder they were laughing. They weren't telling jokes in there, they were laughing at you Benny, that's what they were doing. Laughing at you and how pathetic you are.

Ben pressed his palm to the side of his head, clenching his teeth. Stop it! stop it you hear! Get out!

Feeling angry with himself and realising this was a complete waste of time – he wasn't going to see a thing either, he backed away from the tent and out of the field, cursing under his breath as he staggered down the road. His stomach churned now and he thought he might be sick, and that bloody migraine – that's what he thought it was – was coming back again. Just needed to lie down for a bit, that's all – then he'd be fine after a good night's sleep.

Bitches! Laughing at him. He'd show them what he was made of. When the time was right. Just like the last one he'd done away with.

He'd bloody well kill them.

SIX

Maddie woke to the sound of birds chittering in the trees and hedgerows. She opened her eyes. The pitch blackness had gone and daylight now permeated the mesh material of the tent just enough so she could see inside. She stifled a yawn, tried sitting up and slumped back down again. How could she forget she was trapped in a sleeping bag? And the term 'packed in like sardines' came too her then. Feeling for the zip inside, she opened the bag down as far as her knees and sat up. Maddie stretched her limbs and yawned again, her lower back protesting with a dull ache as she arched backward. The combination of carrying a weight and sleeping on a two-inch piece of bedroll was already making itself felt, but she was sure the stiffness would go away once she got moving again.

Unzipping the bag all the way to her ankles she brought her knees back, hugging them while she reached down to massage her feet and toes. She half expected to feel some residual soreness left over from yesterday but there was only a slight stiffness in her ankles when she flexed her feet. At least that was something she thought, as she swung her legs around and placed her feet on the ground sheet.

Jodie's sleeping bag moved. 'Morning,' she said, sitting up and yawning. She looked like she'd been dragged backwards through a bush, her unkempt curly hair appearing even more bedraggled than normal. 'Sleep well?'

'Better than I thought.' Maddie lifted her arms and sniffed tentatively under her armpits. 'Surprised I don't stink!'

Jodie stretched out her arms and yawned loudly. 'Don't worry. You will by the end of the day.'

'Thanks. I could murder a shower right now.'

'Oh well, once mums picked us up the day after tomorrow you can have one at mine. In the meantime, the only person smelling you right now is me and as I probably smell the same I won't hold it against you. Okay?

'Thanks.' Maddie said flatly, rubbing the sleep from her eyes and stifling yet another yawn.

Jodie started to unzip her own bag. 'Anyway –

you know what they say?'

'What's that?'

'Pigs don't smell their own shit.'

'Ha ha. It's not the pigs I'm worried about – its everyone else. I must stink to high heaven. They'll smell me a mile away.'

The two girls broke into laughter before deciding they had better get a move on if they wanted to reach Bodmin by the early afternoon. The thirteen miles would take them at least five to six hours – including a couple of rest stops – and if they left by nine they should be there by tea time. Before getting dressed Maddie made sure to spray her body with plenty of deodorant. Especially under her arms.

They had breakfast in the village café, both girls taking the opportunity to use the toilet and give their faces a quick wash. Maddie had thought about taking her wash bag with her and having a strip wash in the sink, but realised it wasn't fair to keep other customers waiting to use the loo. Not that the café had been busy at that time of the morning. There'd only been a few people in there; a young couple that looked like they were still in the honeymoon period as they never seemed to tear their eyes away from each other, a man in paint spattered dungaree's that could only be a painter and decorator and some bloke in a bright red baseball cap sat in the opposite corner, who

Maddie thought looked a little bit shifty. Jodie wasn't keen on the idea anyway, telling her they risked being chucked out if they got caught semi-naked in the public loo, not to mention the embarrassment it would cause.

It was after nine when they left the village behind, both girls feeling invigorated now after a good night's sleep and a hearty cooked breakfast, and it wasn't long before the stiffness of the previous day's exertions had been shaken from their limbs.

They passed the field they had stayed in last night, following the narrow road until they came to the sign for the Copper Moor Trail again. Striding out alongside Jodie, Maddie could already feel the morning sunlight caressing her face and she was glad she had put on a vest and shorts this morning instead of the long-sleeved tee shirt and jeans she had worn yesterday. Jodie was wearing something similar. It wasn't that the weather was hot: warm but with no breeze to cool them they just hadn't figured on how much the exertion would make them perspire, especially carrying a backpack. It was a vicious circle. The more they sweated the more they had to replace fluids with gulps of water from the bottles they carried, Maddie quickly realising if she couldn't have a proper wash the least she could do was try to keep sweating to a minimum by wearing as little as possible. She hoped it didn't get any warmer. Even an increase of two or three degrees could make things a lot more uncomfortable, particularly down there in her feminine regions. Thankfully, her period wasn't due for another two weeks; that would have been too much to handle. Still, Maddie wouldn't say no to a shower or a nice hot bath right now.

They'd left the village over two hours since and hadn't met a single person. Now, coming down the trail at a leisurely pace they saw two people on horseback and the girls pulled in to the side of the track as the riders drew close. They wanted to give them plenty of room, mindful that horses could easily be spooked. Horse riders were a common sight around Cornwall – more so during the summer months – and not just confined to the off beaten track either, catching the unprepared motorist sometimes by surprise as they came around a corner a little too fast. The riders greeted them with a smile and a 'good morning' disappearing quickly out of sight when their broke their animals into a gentle canter.

Further along the track they came across some presents left by the horses, already swarming with disgusting looking flies and the two girls had to step carefully around the massive looking dollops. Jodie said wouldn't it be funny if the law changed meaning horse owners would have to pick up their animal's poop and take it with them, just like dog walkers had to. They both laughed when Maddie said they'd need a bloody big bag and a shovel.

'So?' Jodie started to ask, glancing at her friend. 'Met any fit blokes at that university of yours? And don't tell me you haven't noticed.'

Maddie giggled. 'Yep - there's a few. But you know me Jodie. Getting this degree is more important to me than anything else. I don't need any distractions no matter how fit they are.'

'If you say so.' Jodie smiled.

'Anyway, what about you?

Jodie wore a coy expression. 'What about me?

'You bitch – you are seeing someone, aren't you? I could see it in your face.'

'I might be.'

'You are, aren't you? Come on then, spill the beans. Who is he?'

'It's nothing serious. He's called Ryan if you must know. He's twenty-two and he's in the navy.'

Maddie grinned. 'You know what they say about sailors don't you?'

'One in every port you mean? Yes, I know about all that. But as I said, it's not serious. Only been seeing him a couple of months anyway. At the moment, he's sailing around the Mediterranean somewhere sunning himself.'

'Alright for some. How longs he away for?'

'Six bloody months,' Jodie exclaimed.

'Oh. I can see why you're taking it steady then,

and why you kept it to yourself.' There was no admonishment in her tone. 'Just a bit of fun, eh?'

'Don't get me wrong Maddie. He's nice enough and really good looking, but I'm just not sure I could put up with seeing someone only twice a year...'

Maddie pulled up suddenly. The dappled browns of fern and green gorse, dotted with yellow headed flowers had provided natures camouflage for the short standing stones that sat only a few hundred feet away, and if it hadn't been for the single shadow cast by the tallest stone against the sparse area of grassland Maddie realised she might have missed them altogether.

'What's that over there?' she pointed out.

Jodie looked across, squinting her eyes against the sunlight. 'Don't know,' she said, pulling out her map. 'Let's see.'

She looked towards the stones then down to the map. 'No – they're not on here, unless I'm going blind.' She double checked, then shook her head. 'Nope. They're definitely not marked.'

'Shouldn't they be on the map?'

Jodie slid the map into her back pocket. 'Not necessarily, no. There's lots of them on the moor and only the more important ones would be marked, like the Hurlers, the Piper's or points of interest like Brown Willy Tor.'

'The highest point in Cornwall?' Maddie

remarked, remembering that was Brown Willy's claim to fame and an important landmark that guaranteed its place on any map of Bodmin Moor. Translated from the Cornish, it meant Hill of Swallows, but she couldn't recall exactly how high it was. But as for the stones she had just seen?

Jodie was just as curious as Maddie. 'We can take a look if you want? It's not that far.'

'Okay,' Maddie happily agreed.

The moor combined flat grassy plains, favoured by grazing animals, and more difficult undulating terrain, often hiding rabbit holes beneath thick tussocks and ferns that could easily twist an ankle to the unobservant walker. Streams and natural ponds were also in abundance, as well as marshes, bogs and wet meadows that held their own hidden dangers to the unwary. At all costs, the wetland areas were best avoided altogether and had claimed more than their fair share of shoes from startled owners as they struggled ankle deep in the sucking mud. That's if you were lucky. Deeper areas were potentially life threatening, especially if you were foolish to go there alone. Waist high in a bog was almost impossible to escape from. Where they were headed was thankfully flat grassland and they made the short journey in under five minutes, Maddie excited at the prospect of what they might find.

As they drew close they saw there were three

stones that formed a rough triangle. Maddie stood in the middle and playfully stretched her arms out sideways in a gesture to reach them, but her fingertips fell short a good foot either side. Height wise they came up to her chin, shorter than the Hurlers at Minions village and the girls walked all the way around, looking at them and wondering what significance they might once have had.

Maddie touched one, running her fingers lightly over the granites rough speckled surface, lingering perhaps a little too long as if she were perhaps waiting for the stone to offer up some mystical insight into its ancient past. Hadn't she seen that in a movie once; the legend of Stonehenge or something? But nothing other worldly came to her, not that she really expected it to.

Just then a group of wild ponies came into view from across the moor. They passed the stones at a distance, frolicking as they went, occasionally stopping to graze on the lush grass that carpeted that particular area of moorland. Although they were too far away to get meaningful photographs the girls took them anyway.

They decided to stop here and have an early lunch. Maddie slid the backpack off, letting it fall to the ground and the relief was instant. It reminded her of that dead heavy feeling of your body when you climbed out of the swimming pool, except this was the opposite way around.

They sat in the triangle, resting against the stones, snacking on crisps and some chocolate, washed down with bottled mineral water they'd bought in the village store earlier that morning.

'Ouch!' Maddie flinched, slapping her neck with her palm. 'Something just bit me!' She stared in disbelief at the tiny spot of blood on her finger. She had killed the culprit though. It lay squashed on her thigh where it had fallen, and she flicked it off in disgust.

'Horse fly I bet.' Jodie remarked, indicating a pile of horse manure a few feet away.

'Little sod! That stung.' She checked her neck again. No blood this time. 'Is there a mark?'

Jodie scrambled over and Maddie tilted her head. 'It's only a scratch. Lucky for you it must have been a little one. They can leave a painful red bump. I've been bitten myself a few times around the farm.'

'Just a baby vampire then,' Maddie managed to joke, as Jodie sat down opposite her again, leaning against one of the stones.

'We'd better not hang around here too long,' said Jodie. 'Don't fancy getting sucked to death.'

Maddie looked around for signs of anymore horseflies. Or anything that flew, come to that, but it seemed they were more interested in the pile of horse poo, judging by the swarm. Well, as long as they stayed over there. She kept an eye out, ready to swat anything that dared come her way.

'Found anything interesting?' Maddie asked, in between chewing a square of chocolate.

Jodie had her knees up, map open across them. 'Something I saw earlier. There's a path showing here that branches away from the main trail. It looks like it cuts straight across the moor then links up with the trail again.'

'So – what you thinking?' Maddie had an inkling, but was too busy savouring the velvety texture of the chocolate as it melted and coated the inside of her mouth.

'There's nothing much to see between here and where that path joins up with the trail, so if we took the short cut it could save us maybe forty minutes or so. We'd definitely get to Bodmin by tea time.'

Maddie nodded, clearing her palate with her tongue. 'If it means less time carrying that thing then it sounds good to me,' she responded gratefully, eyeing her pack that seemed a tad heavier and less forgiving over the last few miles.

'To be honest we've lost a bit of time stopping here anyway, and I don't know if you've noticed, but we've got some cloud coming in over there.'

Maddie looked over her shoulder. 'Where did that come from?'

Against the vast expanse of blue she could now

see a thin white bank of cloud hanging ominously low on the horizon. It hadn't been there minutes ago, or perhaps she hadn't noticed it. *'Before you know it, a mist can come down in no time.'* She shooed the memory away, like she did the time her neighbour's cat had snuck into her garden recently and was preparing to pounce on the tiny unsuspecting bird she'd been feeding with breadcrumbs. There was nothing unusual in what the old lady had said, even the guide book had mentioned how unpredictable the weather could be. And hadn't the waitress said more or less the same thing? It was common knowledge from those that knew of the moors reputation and her imagination was just cooking up a forewarning that simply wasn't there. It was as simple as that.

'British weather, eh.' Jodie said, cynically.

Maddie broke off another piece of chocolate, holding it close to her lips. 'Okay, let's take the shortcut. What's the worst that can happen?'

'It gets cloudier, chucks it down and we get soaked to the skin. Then a mist comes down and we get lost out here.'

'Be careful what you wish for...'

'Because you might just get it,' Jodie chimed, finishing the sentence. 'Yes – I know, I shouldn't tempt fate, should I?'

'No, you shouldn't. Anyway, good job I packed my rain jacket then, isn't it? But I forgot me wellies.'

Jodie was getting to her feet now. 'Me too,' she laughed. 'I wouldn't worry about it though, I don't think it'll come to that – come on, we'd better get a move on.'

As they walked back to the trail Maddie pulled out her phone, almost forgetting she could use it to check the weather forecast. They had abstained from using their phones except for emergencies and to check for any text messages they might have received. There was no way the batteries would last for three days if they constantly fiddled with them and they'd agreed to switch them off in the evening to conserve the batteries.

A look of dismay came over her when she saw the phone was displaying the last weather report she'd looked at before leaving home. It was frozen on Plymouth and it suddenly dawned on her the phone needed access to the internet. There was no wi-fi out here! Jodie's would be the same as they were both on the same network. Bummer, she thought, but at least her battery was eighty percent full. The signal wasn't good though; just two green bars.

When they reached the main trail again, Jodie consulted her map which told her the path should just be up ahead on their left. When they got there, they saw the path wasn't signposted and it snaked out across flatter terrain before disappearing at a point in the distance where the landscape undulated. Except for the occasional bird song or the distant wavering cry of a sheep from somewhere across the moor, it was perfectly quiet and Maddie had to asked herself if this was perhaps the calm before the storm? As she set foot on the path Jodie started to sing. 'Here we go – here we go – here we go...' Maddie joining in the fun as she fell in alongside her friend.

'If anyone could see us now,' Maddie said, looking around. 'They'd think we were a couple of fruit cakes, wandering across the moor and singing our heads off.'

'Ha, they probably would, wouldn't they? Like the two hikers in the werewolf movie.'

'Eh?'

'That film. An American Werewolf in London. Didn't they start singing something or other after hearing the werewolf?'

'Did they?'

'When they left the Slaughtered Lamb and it was dark and it started to rain. Remember? It put the fear of god into them when they heard it howling like that and I'm sure they started singing to settle their nerves. Or maybe I'm wrong?'

'Can't remember to be honest,' Maddie said. 'Great. And here we are tempting fate. Again!' The last word was stressed.

'With our dulcet tones, it would frighten the

local cats away.'

'Speak for yourself,' Maddie chided. 'I used to sing in the local church choir, don't you remember?'

'Yeah! When you were twelve,' Jodie chuckled.

Their light-hearted banter was cut short when they heard the land rover approaching. It was crossing the moor to their left, its engine roaring louder the closer it got to them. The driver lurched to a halt, engine ticking in idle, thick clouds of diesel smoke billowing from the rear. The window was down and they saw an older man wearing a flat cap, crow's feet around his eyes and weathered features who looked like a typical farmer.

'Afternoon,' he said flatly. 'Hope you don't mind me saying, but the weathers on the change you know.'

'Oh,' Maddie said, looking at Jodie.

'I know it might not look it now, but trust me, I've got sheep out here and I know these moors like a moody child. Been farming out here all my life. Where are you headed?'

'Bodmin,' Jodie replied.

'Hmm,' he said, scratching the stubble on his chin. 'I'm not going that way, but I can drop you back at the trail if you like?'

'Oh – thanks anyway, but we're fine,' Jodie said firmly.

'We've got our wet weather gear,' Maddie

added. 'Thanks though.' She gave a brief smile, not wishing to offend.

'Okay – if you're sure? Just thought I'd ask. I haven't seen another soul out here for hours though, so take care okay.'

He slipped the rover into gear, but before pulling away stuck his head out the window again. 'Take my advice. If you get lost out here just follow a stream and it'll lead you off the moor. They all do eventually. Take care now.'

He drove off quickly, crossing the path in front of them, the stench of diesel fumes hanging in the air.

They looked at each other quizzically before Maddie asked, 'Do you think we should have taken him up on his offer?'

Jodie shook her head. 'No – we'll be okay. He'd have taken us all the way back to where we started, and we've lost enough time as it is.'

Ambling alongside, Maddie said: 'Yes, I suppose so.' They must have been on this path for over an hour and going back would have been pointless. All they had to do was keep to it as planned and everything would be fine. They'd be in Bodmin in no time at all.

'He was right about one thing though,' Maddie said. 'Except for those horse riders, we haven't seen anybody else for ages. It's almost like we're the only ones out here.'

'Oh, I doubt that. It's just that the moor is so vast, that's all, and we have left the main trail, haven't we?'

'Hmm, if you say so.' Maddie sounded unconvinced.

Noting that Maddie was comfortably matching her stride, Jodie increased the pace just a little. If the farmer was right and the weather was about to change for the worst, then there was no point hanging about. She glanced at her friend. 'Anyway, for all we know he could have been a nutcase, couldn't he? Like that lunatic in that Aussie film who rescues those kids after their car breaks down but they don't realise he's a raving psycho until he drugs them and ties them up in his cellar...'

Maddie nodded. Unlikely, but possible. You heard all sorts of stories about hikers on their own. Especially females. Like that couple who were backpacking around the Australian outback and had been abducted and held for days by some maniac before managing to escape. And then there was the other weirdo she had seen on the news. Germany or Switzerland, she couldn't remember which. Hadn't he abducted a young woman and held her in chains in his cellar for months? This wasn't the outback, sure, but even so? Stuff like that happened in this country too. She remembered the man in the ticket booth; the letch, and instantly felt glad that they'd refused the farmers offer. No – they'd made the right decision, Maddie thought.

Jodie's watch showed one pm. The map in her hand told her that Bodmin was roughly six miles away, so provided they didn't dawdle or stop along the route they should be there by four-thirty at the latest.

'Is this a race?' Maddie asked, realising she was struggling to keep up. Although not out of breath, she imagined she might be any time soon if she had to keep this up.

'God no – I can go faster than this,' she said wittily.

'Err – no, this'll do fine.' Despite the thinly veiled reply Maddie wasn't about to complain because she knew exactly why her friend had suddenly upped the pace. The sky wasn't looking so cheerful anymore, that light grey bank of cloud she'd seen earlier now appearing dark and broody on the distant horizon.

SEVEN

Ben felt like shit when he woke up, but at least the headache had gone now. He stumbled across the darkened bedroom into the cramped bathroom opposite and ran some cold water, cupping the liquid in both hands before splashing his face. Feeling for the hand rail on the wall, he grabbed a grubby towel and used it to dab around his weasel like eyes and the rest of his gaunt looking features.

He scratched at the stubble on his chin and stuck his tongue out in the mirror above the sink. Yuck. His mouth felt like somebody had taken a crap there recently, but he couldn't smell his own stale cigarette breath any more than if it had been a heavy garlic dinner he'd eaten the night before. Only other people would notice that, if they got close enough.

He'd had a few too many last night, hadn't he? The bloodshot eyes peering back at him now had a couple of dark circles for company, evidence of too much alcohol and a restless night's sleep. Well, what do you expect, eh Benny? Your mother was a bleedin alky wasn't she? That's where you get it from. Runs in the family doesn't it. This time the annoying voice in his head was right about one thing, but only one. She'd knock back a bottle of vodka a day when she could afford it, which wasn't that often. The rest of the time a couple of bottles of cheap wine would do the trick or anything else that would satisfy her craving. As she became more and more drunk, he'd learned it was better to get out the way, either go to his room or just nip down the park with his football before dad got home. Before the arguments began. Before he got in the way and felt the back of his dad's hand simply because she'd made him so angry. Ben just wanted all of it to go away. If it hadn't been for the school dinners he'd looked forward to during the week it could be pot luck for him in the hot meal stakes. That's if she was capable of standing long enough to make one or if she could even be bothered too. Yet, to her credit, she always managed to find something in her purse and he would quite happily trot off to the takeaway for a bag of chips and a battered sausage. Sometimes he'd scoff the lot on the way back, but most of the time he'd sit on the bench in the park waiting until it was safe to go home and the war between his parents had subsided.

But he wasn't in the same league as an alcoholic, he kept telling himself. He never touched spirits, despising the burning taste of whisky and bacardi and only drank pints of lager. Surely, that didn't make him one of them.

He padded back to the bedroom and had to scramble about the room looking for his jeans and tee shirt he'd discarded last night. He felt hungry now. After a drinking session he'd be ravenous and grab a takeaway from the chippie, eating it on his short journey home. But last night had been different, hadn't it? The chippie was shut and he just wanted to fall into bed and make the headache go away. What he needed right now was a nice big fry up to soak up all the booze he'd had last night. Some bacon, eggs and fried bread in the village café would do the trick. But there was something else he had to do first.

Lighting up a half smoked roll up he'd stuck in his mouth, he strolled into the kitchen, pulled open a drawer and took out a familiar black handled object. Holding it up in front of him he pressed the little button on the side of the handle and the blade sprung open with an ominous click. Dragging hard on the roll up, he filled the small kitchen with smoke before sticking it between his lips again and letting it hang. A grin spread over his face as he twisted his wrist and the blade glinted in the harsh light cast by the single unshaded light bulb hanging above. Closing the flick knife with both hands he slid it into his back pocket before leaving the cottage.

It was bright and sunny when he strolled past the field, expecting to see their tent sitting there when he peered over the gate. But there was only one, and it wasn't the one he'd stood outside of last night. He felt a mixture of anger and disappointment. Mostly anger. They had gone already and given him the slip. Ben had been tricked. Outsmarted by a couple of girls, his little plan he'd been some meticulous over now unravelling in front of him. Thought they were clever, did they? Pulling a fast one on him... But they couldn't have gotten that far, could they? Unless they'd left in the middle of the night which was highly unlikely. They'd probably got up at the crack of dawn, he thought, but that would have been a couple of *hours ago, at least. Damn! He suspected they were following the Copper Moor Trail – every other hiker coming through here did – he just didn't know which direction they were heading. It was either Bodmin or the opposite direction to Minions. But whichever way they were going they couldn't have gotten too far with those packs they were carrying and he just might be able to catch up with them if he got a move on. Anyway, he reasoned they'd be in no great rush, stopping now and again to take in the sights that made the trail so popular with hikers. Yes – of course they would, he convinced himself. Panic over. But which way? First though, he needed something to eat. If he was going to catch them. He couldn't do it on an empty stomach.*

Ben pushed open the café door and when he spotted blondie and butch sitting there in the far corner – the bigger girl had her back to him – his stomach did a somersault and he half considered turning right around just then and walking away. But that would have looked funny, wouldn't it? That would have really made him stand out. Anyway, he couldn't do that because Lizzy behind the counter had glanced up to see who was entering and had given him a brief smile. It was too late now. Luckily blondie hadn't looked his way because she was too busy looking at the menu in front of her. At least that was something.

He headed for the empty table on the other side of the room, all the time looking out the corner of his eye but neither girl noticed him. It would have helped if the café had been busier, allowing him to go better unnoticed in a room full of diners, but it was early yet and he hadn't counted on them being here.

Lizzy came to his rescue just then. She was by their table now, taking their order. Brilliant! He swiped a discarded newspaper from one of the empty tables as he passed and before he sat down pulled his cap down a tad, shading his eyes. So far so good.

What had at first seemed like a disaster didn't seem half as bad now. He'd thought they'd got away and here they were right in his sights again. Now, if that wasn't fate favouring him, he didn't know what was. All he had to do was act normal and keep a low profile and everything would turn out just fine. It couldn't have worked out better. The twisted satisfaction he felt knowing he'd been stood so close to their tent last night and here they were only feet away again, not having a bloody clue about any of it – well – it was like a massive adrenaline rush and he was in complete control of it. Of course, he had the power to stop it any time he wanted. But he was revelling in it now and that wasn't going to happen – not yet – not until he'd got what he wanted and not until he decided it was over. He chuckled. At least he could take his time now and enjoy a nice breakfast. They had only just ordered theirs.

'What'll it be Ben. You want the usual?'

He looked up from the newspaper and into the familiar chubby face hovering over him. She was chewing gum, as usual.

'Yeah, the all-day will be fine,' he said, forcing a smile. 'And I'll have some toast with that too.'

He'd known her since school, and she hadn't changed a bit. Lard ass Lizzy he used to call her. She still was, but he'd never said it to her face though. And as far as he could remember she hadn't called him Benny either. Not like the others. But, it hadn't stopped her thinking it though. Maybe she had.

'You want coffee? You look like you could use it – late night was it?'

The last four words bothered him. What did she mean by that? And for one awful moment he thought his clever little plan had been blown out the water and she'd been watching *him last night as he stood outside the girls tent in the middle of the field. But that's not what she meant, was it? She couldn't have seen him in the pitch darkness anyway. He felt like telling her to mind her own bloody business and just go get him his coffee but he just smiled back thinly.*

'Yeah – something like that.' He had to stop himself from sneering. 'I'll need some extra sugar too. Last time I came in here they only gave me one sachet. That's about half a teaspoon. No wonder the coffee tasted bitter.'

Lard ass Lizzy stopped chewing and her cheeks flushed red. 'Oh, sorry to hear that,' she apologised. 'I'll make sure to bring you some extra. Okay, the all-day breakfast with toast and coffee. Thank you. Be right back.'

He watched her butt as she turned and waddled off. Lard ass, he thought, then had to stop himself from laughing aloud when he imagined he could probably slide a bike wheel between those ass cheeks and use her as a stand. But she'd probably enjoy it, he chuckled to himself, reckoning that would be the only thing anyone would want to slide between there. Fat bitch!

As he waited for his coffee and food he listened to the snippets of conversation drifting across from the other side of the room. He couldn't hear everything, but enough to learn they'd been following the Copper Moor Trail because Butch had mentioned Minions village and something about the Hurlers stone circle they'd taken some pictures of. And it was then that Ben laughed to himself. They'd already been there then, hadn't they, so they must be heading for Bodmin after all. He couldn't believe his luck. Everything was falling nicely into place.

He knew the moor like the back of his hand having spent the past twenty years or so as a general labourer cum handy man. Anything that needed doing he would do it and it was mostly stuff people couldn't be bothered to do or simply didn't have the time for: house clearance, garden and general waste disposal, farm work, to name just a few. Being self-employed was handy indeed for he could pick and choose his jobs and the days he worked. And the days he liked to watch the women. Now, that really helped. Like this weekend for example. Ben was going to have himself some fun for a change, now that he'd taken the first two steps. There was no going back now.

'One coffee.' Lard ass Lizzie placed the mug on the table. She reached into her apron pocket and pulled out a handful of sugar sachets. 'Four be enough?'

He looked up into her piggy eyes, the bottom half of her face in constant motion as she chewed gum, and down to the chubby fingers holding the little bags of sugar. Her pink painted fingernails suited her perfectly and Ben made pig sounds inside his head. Oink! Oink! Did she realise just how ugly and stupid she looked?

'Yeah, great. Four's fine.' He took them, turned back to the newspaper and started tearing at the sachets, making it obvious he didn't want any chit chat. Not today anyway.

She waddled off again, disappearing behind the counter.

The scraping of chair legs from the other side of the room grabbed his attention and he glanced over coyly to see Blondie getting up from the table. She was wearing a skimpy pink vest and khaki shorts and they looked pretty good on her, he thought, as he watched her nubile form cross the room and enter the toilets. She was a looker alright. Nineteen or twenty perhaps? The pair of them didn't look much older than that.

He peeked over at Butch and saw she too was wearing shorts and a vest, her broad shoulders, muscular upper arms and thick thighs more in evidence without the benefit of the jeans and tee shirt she'd worn yesterday.

She could be a shot putter with a body like that, he thought, or even a wrestler. Yes, that's it, a mud wrestler and a lewd image formed in his mind of her rolling around in the mud in a bikini, cavorting with an equally formidable looking female. Ha ha, he'd like to see that. He saw she was busy fiddling with her phone. At least she was distracted, thank god. The last thing he needed was her looking around the room and eye balling him while she waited for her friend to return. She looked up when lard ass Lizzie appeared with their food and he watched her bending over slightly as she set their plates down. Her backside looked twice as big now. Oink! Oink! Miss piggy, he smirked inside, wondering what the hell Kermit ever saw in her anyway.

When lard ass Lizzie brought his breakfast over and placed it on the table in front of him, blondie came out of the toilet and re-joined her mud wrestling friend.

Ben finished his breakfast about the same time the girls were getting up to leave and when he saw them exit the café he ambled over to the counter and paid for his breakfast. Take your time, he'd told himself. There was no need to rush – he knew which way they were headed anyway – and he didn't want to give any impression to lard ass Lizzy over

129

there that he was in any kind of hurry. It could come back to haunt him, couldn't it? Questions like 'Did she remember who was in the café when the girls were here? Was anyone acting suspiciously or out the ordinary? Did anyone follow them out? No – that wouldn't do. Just take your sweet little time and act normal. Don't draw any attention to yourself Ben, like he'd told himself a thousand times before. Everything would work out just fine.

Ben made sure to keep his distance. Although it was common to see walkers on the trail he didn't want them spotting him no matter how innocent it looked. If they looked back for any reason and saw him they might become suspicious as to why he was holding back and never seemed to catch up or overtake them. A man on his own, especially so. It wasn't difficult to imagine their conversation.

'Have you noticed that guy behind us?'

'Yeah, I saw him.'

'He's been following us since we left the village.'

'I know.'

'Don't you think it's kinda funny. I mean – he doesn't look like a hiker or anything. What do you think he's doing all the way out here?'

'I don't know. The only thing we can do is

take a rest stop, see what he does.'

'I don't like it.'

No. They wouldn't like it, would they? He'd have to be extra careful.

There were a few disused mine workings dotted all over the place but he knew they'd only prove useful if they were close to hand when he needed somewhere to hide quickly, and trees were sparse on this section of the moor leaving gorse bush and natural dips in the ground the only real cover available.

Ben had to stop on the trail when he saw them pull up to allow some riders on horseback past and he realised they'd reach him in no time at all when he saw them suddenly break into a canter. He scrambled behind a thick area of gorse and waited there until it was safe to come out again. Of course, he knew he couldn't avoid everyone but the less people that saw him out here the better. And it wasn't too long after when he had to hang back again as he watched them cross the moor towards the three standing stones where they stayed for a while and had something to eat. He'd thought this might be it. This could be his chance, and he'd watched them like a hawk, hoping they might separate but they stayed together the whole time. No such luck.

He kept well out of sight until they returned

to the trail and as they moved off he started shadowing them, being careful to keep a safe distance again.

But his stealthiness couldn't help him avoid the vehicle that appeared out of nowhere, the noise from its engine muffled by the dip in the ground as it crested the hillock in front of him. Shit, he thought, recognising who the blue land rover belonged to. It was distant enough that there was every chance the driver hadn't spotted him yet, so he turned around quickly and walked in the opposite direction, making out he was heading for the village. With any luck, he'd got away with it.

He pulled up at the side of the trail as the land rover squealed to a halt beside him. The driver stuck his head out.

'Hey Ben!' The farmer wasn't that surprised to see him out here. Ben was always out and about doing something or other, although he half expected to see a shotgun in his hand or some dead rabbits slung over his shoulder.

'Alright John,' he greeted the older man, feigning surprise. He'd done a few odd jobs for him over the years and helped him mend some fences recently. Always paid cash in hand, no questions asked and he was worth keeping in with.

'Not shooting today then?'

Ben didn't need to think fast. When he'd heard the rover he already knew the reason he would give for being out here. 'No – not today, just checking on some snares, that's all.'

He stuck his hands casually into the front pockets of his jeans, aware now that he should have brought something meaningful along that inferred anything other than the little stroll he was taking. Idiot! An empty sack for the rabbits would have been a good idea. But it was too late for that. Hold your nerve Benny, the voice in his head said.

The farmer nodded. 'No luck then I see?'

'Nope. Not today. Not a damn thing,' he laughed, kicking himself for his lack of foresight.

The farmer chortled. 'You must be losing your bloody touch Ben. No rabbit stew for you tonight then?' he jibed.

Bloody ha ha, Ben thought. I'll put you in a stew, sarcastic prat. But he just smiled back thinly and chose not to reply.

'Anyway, I'm glad I bumped into you.'

'Oh.'

'I could use a hand sometime when your free. There's a few jobs I keep meaning to get on with – but you know how it is, eh?

'Yeah, I know,' Ben agreed, relieved that

the conversation had moved on and the farmer had swallowed his lie. 'Can't do next week I'm afraid. I promised old Mrs Tomkins I'd make a start on her back garden. Like a bloody jungle back there so it is. Can't put her off again.'

'No, no, of course not.' He knew the eighty-year-old woman had no family and her frailty meant she had to rely on the help of others. Ben had done quite a few odd jobs for the old biddy over the years. A few that some in the village said she didn't really need doing. It was well known that the old dear wasn't short of a bob or two, having retired years ago on a pension from the headmistress position she'd held at the local primary school as well as a generous life insurance payment she'd received when her husband had died at the age of seventy-two. They'd accused Ben of fleecing her; making up jobs that didn't exist, but they'd never said it to his face though. Not directly. He had a temper if you got on the wrong side of him, according to some, although to be fair he hadn't seen any evidence of it himself. As far as he knew it could all be hogwash; sour grapes, and he'd give him the benefit of doubt until he learnt otherwise. Like he did with everyone.

Keen to move things along, Ben said. 'Should only take me a few days to sort it out.

I can be with you the week after next if that's any good to you?'

'That'll do just fine,' he replied. 'Give you a lift back to the village if you like. Looks like the weathers about to turn by the look of it.'

The gloominess on the horizon hadn't been lost on him. 'Yeah – could be your right, but I'll take my chances if you don't mind. Anyway, I could do with the exercise.' He gave him a steely look.

'Suit yourself. Don't know what's wrong with everybody today though?'

'What do you mean?'

He jerked his head back. 'Couple of hikers back there. Off the main trail they were. Thought I was doing them a favour but they didn't want a lift either. Mind you, can't say I really blame them and all – two girls out on their own in the middle of nowhere and me being a stranger and all.'

'Hikers you say?'

'Yeah, a couple of young women. Looked like they were taking the shortcut across the moor. I tried warning them about the weather.'

'Ah right,' Ben said, trying to appear indifferent. 'But that's tourists for you. They think they know better than the rest of us, don't they?'

'That might be true, but we need their

money, don't we? And if they want to tramp around the moor all day without any heed of the dangers, then that's fine by me. Can't say I didn't warn them though.'

Ben just nodded coolly.

'Anyway, can't hang around here chatting all day. Things to do.' He put the rover in gear. 'See ya Monday week, about nine?'

It sounded more like an instruction than a statement, Ben thought. 'See you then.'

As he drove away Ben thought he'd needed that chance encounter like a hole in the head, especially now the farmer had told him about the two bitches back there. More bloody questions. 'Did you see anyone else on the moor near to where the girls were? Ben Smith knew about the hikers because you told him, eh? He didn't get a lift back with you?

A familiar voice popped into his head again. Now that's torn it Benny. You can bet your sweet ass Mr farmer back there will be the first to come forward if anything happens to those girls. And when he does, you better be ready and have a damn good alibi because he's bound to mention you, isn't he? He wouldn't want anyone pointing the finger of suspicion at him, not if you could help back up his story. Well, you better watch your back. You mark my words Benny, you really didn't *need that. Its messy already and you haven't even done anything yet.*

Ben felt a dull throb in his head, causing him to wince. *Not one those headaches again, not now.* They seemed to be coming more frequently lately. The normal voice in his head took over then. *Why don't you take a running jump? I know what I'm doing and if I want your advice I'll bloody well ask for it. I've been here before, remember? And they didn't catch me then either. Who gives a damn about an alibi anyhow? They'd have to prove it first and without a body they wouldn't have a cat in hells chance. A reasonable doubt, remember, a reasonable doubt and they have to acquit. They can't convict without a body.*

He took a deep breath and the tension he'd felt seemed to lessen its grip on him and when he realised the headache was no longer imminent he turned around – after watching the land rover disappear from view – and hurried along the trail. He didn't want to lose them. Not after he'd come this far.

EIGHT

It came in fast and before they realised it they were cloaked in an impenetrable mist with visibility reduced to a few feet. Even Jodie who was weather wise from working outdoors on the farm, had been surprised by its suddenness. But this was the moor and a completely different landscape than either girl was familiar with. Beautiful and beguiling in summer, unforgiving and desolate in the winter months but also unpredictable and changeable, paying scant regard to the seasons or time of year. Like a five-year-old it could throw a tantrum when you least expected it. And now it had.

Gingerly negotiating the barely visible path now, they half wished they'd taken the farmer up on his offer of a lift despite their earlier reservations. The main trail would have been easier to follow, well-trodden and signposted, with little chance of wandering away from it and getting lost on the moor. But here there was nothing, the path one of many and they could easily take the wrong one. The map was useless if they couldn't see other features on the landscape to help get their bearings from. But Jodie hadn't told Maddie her greatest concern though. A mist could blanket the moors for days, not just a few hours. Of course, Maddie may already know that, but for the moment at least she would spare her that worry. At least it was summer, the mist trapping the warm air and holding it in like a blanket. If it had been the middle of winter, they could have been in real trouble, the combination of the cold and wet and being exposed out here, perhaps proving fatal.

'At this rate,' Jodie said, 'We should reach Bodmin sometime tomorrow night. If we're lucky.'

'That soon?' Maddie quipped.

'Good to see you've still got your sense of humour then?'

Maddie beamed. 'You know me. Always.'

'I think we're going to need our rain jackets,' Jodie said, looking up with arms outstretched and palms facing skyward. 'The farmer was right after all.'

'Oh well – so much for female intuition.' She could feel the moisture in the air now but had dismissed earlier the single droplet that had arrived almost unnoticed on the top of her head.

But when it started to spit, they quickly threw their packs off and rummaged inside for their water proofs. They wasted no time in getting them on and Maddie thought cynically that it was the last item of clothing she expected to be donning in the middle of summer. Jodie's experience during her girl guide years was proving its worth.

'Great!' Maddie said, hoisting her pack on again. 'Now we get wet.' Her tone was light hearted despite her choice of words.

Jodie put her hood up and smiled. 'Just think on the bright side. If you had some soap, you could strip off now and have that nice shower you were looking forward to.'

Maddie eyes widened. 'Now, why didn't I think of that?'

'I see you're not going to let a bit of rain dampen your sense of humour.'

Maddie smiled at the intended pun. 'You're a laugh a minute Jodie.'

'I try my best.'

Starting off again, Jodie surprised Maddie by changing direction, away from the path. Maddie whirled around. 'Where you going?'

Jodie turned on her heels. Her hair was damp and tiny beads of water clung to her face. 'You'll have to trust me Maddie. There's some trees this way – I'm sure there is.'

'Trees?'

'Where that land rover came from earlier. There was a crop of trees behind it. A small wood. Do you remember seeing them?'

Maddie realised she *had* seen a small wooded area, but she hadn't paid much attention at the time. It had been there in the background as the land rover trundled towards them.

'Your right, I remember now, but shouldn't we stick to the path? You said so yourself.'

The spitting had turned to light rainfall and everything became clear to her now. Jodie was taking them to shelter. They could take cover amongst the trees, away from the rain that was getting heavier and heavier and threatening to soak them to the skin. It occurred to her that there was one advantage to the rainfall. As long as it lasted it would keep away the midges and those grotesque looking horse flies.

At least the ground was even, Maddie thought, as they inched their way forward, their progress hampered by the mist and the heavy rain driving into them now, forcing them to keep their heads low to keep the water from entering their hoods. But rain had already found its way inside and Maddie could feel it trickling down the side of her neck and her shorts felt soaked now right through to her knickers. It wasn't a pleasant feeling. What she wouldn't do for a change of dry clothes, she thought, wishing she'd kept her jeans on instead and not have to feel the water running uncomfortably down her legs. But more than anything else, and left unchecked for too long she knew that painful sores could soon develop on the inside of her thighs from the constant friction. Maddie was thankful though that it wasn't a winter rainfall she was having to endure. The chilling affect would have been unbearable and she imagined it would probably have taken her breath away.

She tried to recall how far away the crop of trees had appeared earlier. A few hundred metres maybe; it couldn't have been much farther than that. Were they even heading in the right direction? she found herself wondering. A few feet off, and they could walk right past them in this goddam awful mist and end up wandering around on the moor for hours; if they didn't drown first, she thought cynically. That's if she hadn't already been forced to a halt by those red raw welts that would have stung like a wasp with every stride she took. Like the time she had visited the seaside with mum. When she was little, and the fine sand and sea water had clung to her delicate skin and found its way into every nook and cranny. Even now she could recall vividly how she howled in pain as mum gently tried removing wet grains of sand from between the reddened cracks of her thighs using a soft towel that felt more like sandpaper. The tears had stung her face and only subsided, she fondly remembered, after mum had taken her over to the ice cream van that had made a timely appearance on the beach behind them. By the time she had licked the cornet clean and munched the chocolate flake she always removed first, savouring it until last, the previous agony had diminished.

Her mind was busy now as it played the question and answer game. Too many it seemed. What if the mist hung around all day? Or into the night? She had read that it could stay for days at a time and her meagre supply of crisps and chocolate would have run out by then. But then, you could go without food for weeks, couldn't you? She knew that. It was running out of water you had to worry about. But there were streams on the moor, weren't there? Plenty of running water that was safe to drink and she knew that stagnant or standing water was best avoided as it provided the perfect breeding ground for bacteria or parasites.

Maddie thought there was a good chance that other walkers had also got caught out by the sudden change in the weather, although they hadn't come across many since they'd left the village earlier that morning. *'I haven't seen another soul out here in hours,'* she recalled the words of the farmer. Maybe he'd come back with his land rover and find them having realised they might be in trouble, or at least alert the authorities that he'd seen two young women on the moor before the weather turned. So, didn't it make sense to stay put where the farmer had seen them because that's where any rescue party would begin their search? But, all these questions were just a pointless game that her mind played, because she knew she was kidding herself. He wasn't coming back any time soon. Nobody was. She was getting way ahead of herself? The rain would have to stop sometime though, wouldn't it? And the mist could disappear at any moment, as quickly as it had come, and in no time at all they could be walking right out of here and heading for Bodmin. She was worrying about nothing. Except one thing, and it continued to nag her even though she'd tried telling herself it was all a big coincidence. The old lady on the train had been right all along, but then, so had the waitress and the farmer too. But it wasn't just that, was it? Was Jodie right and had she simply misheard what she *thought* the woman had said before she got off the train...? She dismissed the thought from her mind, despite the strange underlying sense – intuition – call it what you like, that the old lady had been trying to warn her about something, something other than the weather...

'It's got to be this way,' she heard Jodie grumble in front. 'If it wasn't for this damn mist.'

'I'm sure we'll find it soon enough,' Maddie reassured her, sensing the urgency in Jodie's voice and realising that she was probably blaming herself for the situation they were now faced with. After all, it had been her idea to take the detour and if they hadn't they might well have been half way to Bodmin by now. But she couldn't blame Jodie. The thought had never entered her head. Not for one second. No one could have predicted how rapidly the weather could turn, let alone a mist so dense that you could hardly see no more than a few feet away, and it was the first time either of them had experienced anything like it.

Suddenly, as if a veil had lifted before them, vague shapes of trees and foliage began to emerge from the mist, and Maddie felt an instant sense of relief. Not just for herself, but for Jodie who must now be feeling a joyous sense of redemption. The appearance of the wood was almost like finding a lost friend she thought, even though she knew it was just a bunch of trees in the middle of the moor.

They scrambled into the densely-populated copse, instantly feeling respite from the rain as the overhead canopy took the brunt of the downpour. Both girls looked like drowned rats, their hair hanging in tangled strands with water dripping from their ear lobes and the tips of their nose.

Jodie got her pack on the ground, opened the top flap and rummaged through the contents.

'What you doing?' Maddie asked, glad now to get her own pack off as she dumped it onto the damp carpet of decayed leaves and twigs that littered the earth. She shook out her arms ridding the jacket of the water beads that clung to it, much like a wet dog would do after being caught in a downpour.

'I've got an idea.' Jodie pulled out a ground sheet followed by four bungee cords. 'We make a roof,' she added, opening the waterproof material and holding it by one corner. She hooked one end of the bungee cord through the corner eyelet of the sheet, stretched it around the nearest tree and attached the hook to the cord near the same eyelet. It was nice and tight.

Maddie helped when she realised what she was doing, and soon the ground sheet was tied to three other trees and they were standing underneath with their hoods down, the last of the water dripping from their jackets and shorts and running down their legs to their socks and boots.

They stood there for a while, looking out from their position a few feet from the edge of the treeline, seeing nothing but rain spattering the earth and that mist that seemed to be even thicker now and swirling ominously all around them. If ever a film crew needed an outdoor scene for their next horror flick, this had to be up there with the best of them, Maddie thought to herself.

Both girls decided now would be as good a time as any to get out of their wet things and change their clothes. The plastic bin liners Jodie had suggested they bring would prove invaluable now Maddie thought as she removed her boots and was surprised to find her socks were still dry, glad now she'd paid the extra for a decent pair of hiking boots. She peeled off her damp shorts and underwear, and for a moment felt a little self-conscious, aware of her half nakedness as she stood there in the middle of the woods drying between her legs with a towel. She mocked herself when she realised nobody else was around and even if they were they wouldn't be able to see her anyway. The mist was as thick as pea soup. Maddie couldn't understand why anyone would want to join one of those nudist groups or whatever it was they called them. When Jodie asked what was so funny, she told her and they both ended up giggling, Jodie reminding her the only peeping tom they had to worry about now were the sheep and cows or the birds in the trees. It was something to tell her friends at university when she got back though: 'Did I tell you about the time I stripped naked in the woods in the middle of the day?' She could hear the response: 'You didn't! did you Maddie?' It would make a good story when she exchanged banter with her peers on what they got up to on their holidays, and it would raise a few eyebrows amongst the more prudish girls she knew but didn't really have much time for. Still, the look on their faces would give her some amusement, despite her ambivalence towards them.

Maddie had thrown on her jeans and a fresh tee shirt and was about to get her boots on when she heard the crack of a branch. It sounded close. Very close. She looked up.

'Did you hear that Jodie?' she whispered, looking around anxiously but seeing nothing but tree trunks a few feet away and the thick blanket of mist that hid everything beyond. To say she was unnerved was an understatement.

Jodie was sat on her pack and doing up her boot lace when she had flinched at the sound. 'I heard it. Probably an animal.' Although Maddie thought she sounded unperturbed Jodie quickly finished tying her other lace.

'Or somebody else?' Maddie said wide eyed.

Jodie stood, looking about. 'Hello! – is someone there...?'

Maddie half expected to hear a voice call out from beyond the trees or a figure to appear from the mist but only silence came back to them, save for the light fluttering of a few birds as they ascended noisily from the canopy above.

'See? Nothing to worry about. Just an animal, that's all.' Jodie said, shrugging it off. Nonplussed, she sat down on her pack again.

'It sounded pretty loud.' Maddie wasn't entirely convinced. She sat down again and hurriedly pulled on her boots that were damp on the outside. *An animal? Had to be bigger than a fox or a rabbit.* 'What sort of animal were you thinking of?'

'Well, it could be anything to be honest. A stray cow could have wandered in here or a wild pony. Who knows?'

'I suppose so. Maybe even sheep?' Maddie said, feeling slightly better now. *If somebody else was lost out here they would have answered, wouldn't they?*

When they saw the rain wasn't going away any time soon, they sat on their backpacks. They could be in for a long wait and they might as well make themselves as comfortable as possible.

'So, what are we going to do now?' Maddie asked.

'Wait for the rain to stop I suppose, then head back the same way until we reach the path again.'

'And if it doesn't?'

'We could always get the tent up and stay here the night,' Jodie said. 'But we'll be starving come tomorrow morning. Of course, there's no guarantee the rain will have stopped by then either.'

'I know. And by tomorrow afternoon we'll look like stick insects,' Maddie joked. 'God, I could murder a big fat juicy cheese burger right now and a large portion of fries drenched in vinegar and smothered in mayo.' She exaggerated her craving by rubbing her tummy with her hand.

'Oh don't – I could eat a bloody horse,' Jodie admonished her. 'Anyway,' she said, looking at her watch. 'It's two now. Why don't we give it another hour and see if it stops raining? If it doesn't, we'll just go for it anyway. The path runs for about four miles before joining the main trail again, then it's only another two miles to Bodmin.'

'That's a better idea. At least we're dry now but to be honest I'd rather get soaked again than miss the chance of something to eat.'

'Me too.' Jodie agreed.

Maddie knew it would be foolish to stay the night here. She only had some chocolate, a packet of crisps and half a bottle of water left in her pack, and by tomorrow morning they would have gone without a proper meal for twenty-four hours. It was five hours since she'd eaten breakfast and her stomach was growling already. She craved caffeine too. Normally by this time of the day she'd have had three or four cups of the stuff. If they left in the morning and the mist was still down, the six-mile hike could take them well past lunch time instead of the three hours they would expect to do it in under normal weather conditions. They would soon tire carrying a backpack with no food in their bellies and she would certainly have a tumultuous headache by then due to extreme caffeine withdrawal. Perhaps not as bad as a heroine junkie, she reasoned. But close. She could murder a coffee right now. No – staying here was a bad idea. They would rest for an hour and then carry on.

The next hour dragged. Maddie thought it had to be the longest she'd ever had to wait for, longer even than the time she had waited patiently from eight until nine for that letter to drop onto the door mat. The postman always arrived around nine. An important life changing letter that would determine her future one way or the other. At least while she was waiting to hear if she'd got into university, she could pass the time by fiddling with her phone, making a coffee or listening to the news on television, but here in the woods, there was nothing to distract her, nothing to help pass the time. She couldn't even admire the scenery because of the mist. Boredom. It was worse than being in the dentist's when you knew you had to have two teeth out and couldn't wait until you were out of the chair and the numbness in your face had passed. She checked her phone. The weather was still stuck on Plymouth, and there were no messages. Battery was still good but the signal was wavering between one and two bars. That wasn't so good.

Out of boredom Maddie's thoughts turned to the previous day's conversation with the farmhand.

'Just suppose,' she asked Jodie who was looking at her map. 'That there really was a big cat out here...?'

'Uh-uh.'

'Oh – I know what he said about how they'd avoid humans at all costs and all – but what would you do if you *really* did come across one? Out here on the moor I mean?'

Jodie looked up. 'Run as fast as I could. That's what I'd do.'

'No, seriously though. Don't they say that's the worst thing to do? To run?'

Jodie saw that Maddie was serious. 'Your right, yes. It's natural instinct to flee, isn't it? But I guess if it was going to attack, you wouldn't stand much of a chance – I mean you couldn't outrun it, could you?'

'Exactly,' Maddie agreed. 'So, what would you do if you were faced with it for real?'

Jodie put her map away, pondering the question. 'I think the best advice is not to make any sudden movement that might startle the animal or provoke an attack. They do say animals can smell fear, don't they? I'm convinced of that anyway. Dad told me once that he could tell how the cows got really agitated when he delivered them to the slaughterhouse. He said you could see the fear in their eyes, and he had a hell of a job getting some of them out of the lorry and down the ramp. They had to chase one around the yard once: the slaughter men and him. He said the cows could smell the death hanging in the air.'

'That's horrible Jodie,' Maddie cringed. 'I suppose you've seen it for yourself, haven't you?'

Jodie shook her head. 'Nope. Ever since he told me that I've always avoided going with him to the slaughter house. Anyway, that's the advantage of having two older brothers, isn't it? I let them do all the dirty work,' she sniggered.

'Yuck. Don't blame you.'

'Hasn't put you off that juicy beef burger you were taking about?'

'Not until you mentioned that, no. They do say ignorance is bliss, don't they? But the way I feel right now, I could eat anything you put in front of me.'

'Yeah, me too. I could eat an extra-large pizza all to myself.'

'And garlic bread too,' Maddie enthused. Don't forget the garlic bread.'

'Mmmmm. I love garlic bread. God! My stomachs rumbling now.'

'Tell me about it,' Maddie said. 'I think we'd better change the subject, don't you?'

'Yeah, I think your right,' Jodie sighed.

'Anyway – what you were saying before. About staying calm and all that ... but you'd be too petrified to follow some sort of text book advice, wouldn't you?' Maddie tried to imagine how she'd cope if faced with a real life and death scenario but she'd never experienced anything remotely close.

'Of course, but nobody knows for sure how they'd react in a situation like that. It's impossible to imagine. But – they do say not to turn your back on the animal but just walk away slowly in a non-threatening manner. Good advice, if you can hold your nerve.'

'Or make as much noise as possible in the hope of frightening it off.' Maddie said, recalling the documentary she'd seen about a tribe in the African bush who kept a tiger away from their village by banging on dustbin lids with sticks.

'Yes, that's another option. Especially if there was a group of you. But, if you were on your own it would be a different story I bet. Unless you had a shotgun handy.'

Maddie nodded, and as she was gathering her thoughts something more overriding happened that instantly curtailed any further discussion. And it couldn't have been anymore welcome right then.

It had stopped raining. Fifty minutes in, and Maddie felt elated. It was almost like winning the bonus ball.

NINE

It didn't take long to dismantle the roof and before Maddie could even blink Jodie had stashed it away in her backpack. It was nearly three when they walked out of the tree line and onto the moor, relieved now that the rain had finally stopped, and they were on their way again and Maddie soon forgot about the noise in the woods that had given her earlier concern.

Although the mist was still down at least they could make some progress again without worrying about getting drenched Maddie thought, as they headed in the general direction that should hopefully lead them back to the path again. She only hoped the rain would stay away long enough though as she didn't fancy stripping off again in the middle of nowhere to change her soggy clothes.

Everything being well they could be in Bodmin by seven and sitting in a nice pub or café and enjoying a hot meal and some much-needed caffeine. She wasn't sure which she wanted the most now: a hot shower or a plate of fish and chips, but she thought if she had to make a choice then it would have to be the food. Right now, coffee had to be a close third. If she didn't get her fix in the next few hours though it would be number one for certain and never mind the shower.

They came out of nowhere, looming out of the mist and making them appear much larger than they actually were. It caught both girls completely by surprise and they scrambled aside to avoid tripping over them, the equally frightened sheep bleating loudly in their ears and rushing frantically past their legs.

Maddie managed to hop over the woolly oncoming missile when she saw it heading straight between her legs, landing awkwardly on her feet and just keeping her balance despite the jolting backpack threatening to topple her over. Jodie wasn't so lucky. One of them brushed hard against the side of her leg as she side stepped another, the momentum sending her sprawling unceremoniously to the ground. As the last of the sheep disappeared through the mist, Jodie sat up, clutching her knee in both hands. She swore.

Maddie rushed over. 'You okay Jodie? It was

the first time she'd heard her cursing like that and she hoped her friend wasn't badly hurt.

'It's my knee,' she winced. 'Stupid sheep!' It was more frustration than anger in her voice. The vision of being unable to walk properly – or perhaps not at all – had appeared in a flash.

'Don't try getting up,' Maddie said firmly as she positioned herself behind her. 'Let's get your pack off before we do anything.'

With her help, Jodie slipped her arms free from the straps and Maddie pushed the backpack aside.

'Now, can you straighten your leg?

Jodie's hands still clasped her knee as she tried tentatively to extend the limb. The movement was painfully slow and Maddie could almost feel Jodie's discomfort as she grimaced. She hadn't quite managed to extend it fully, but it was good enough.

'That's good,' Maddie reassured her. 'Now back the other way.'

Back she went. Slow again, and got her knee almost touching her chest. 'It can't be that bad or I wouldn't be able to do this. Bloody sore though.'

'Well, that's something to be thankful for. How about standing up. Think you can?' Maddie put her hands out.

'I'll try.'

She grabbed hold of Maddie's hands and despite some grimacing and using Maddie as an anchor she managed to hobble to her feet, most of her weight on her good leg though as she held onto Maddie's shoulder to steady herself. Maddie couldn't help thinking she looked like a kangaroo she had seen at the zoo, bouncing like that. Probably not the best time to share the joke with her though.

'At least you can stand,' Maddie said. She slipped her arm around her. 'Can you put any weight on it?'

Jodie shifted some weight across and the throb she felt made her quickly retract her foot from the ground. Again, she tried. Up and down like a cat pawing a dead bird on the grass, making sure it was dead. Until it was sure. Until she was sure the pain wasn't the result of anything worse and that she could handle it. She looked relieved when she managed to keep her foot down, only half her weight over it though. But that was good.

'It hurts, but it's not too bad. At least it's not twisted,' Jodie finally said. 'It'll be fine.'

'Thank god. You had me worried for a second.' Maddie knew that a badly twisted knee would need hospital treatment and they were about as far away from medical help as you could possibly get. Although realistically they were never that far from help if they needed it because they did have their mobile phones. But having to get air lifted off the moor wasn't exactly the way they wanted their hiking trip to end. Her friends at university would love that if they ever found out. Some of them, anyway. She could see a couple of them tittering in the corridor.

'Did you hear about Maddie's little hiking trip?'

'No. What happened?'

'Her and her mate got flown off the moor after only two days apparently. But we knew she'd be like a fish out of water. She's not the sporty type at all, is she?'

'What was she trying to prove anyway?'

'I know. Hardly surprising she wasn't picked for the rowing team.'

'Or the netball team either.'

Maddie pushed the thought aside. That scenario wasn't going to happen, not if she could help it.

She let Jodie stand unaided but stayed close just in case. 'Do you think you'll be able to walk at all?'

'Only one way to find out.'

Jodie stepped out cautiously, her weight mainly on her good leg and managed a few awkward steps albeit with a noticeable limp. She turned and grinned. 'It won't be a speed march, but I think I can do it. Get me a stick and I'll be fine.'

'It hasn't affected your sense of humour. But your forgetting your backpack – you won't be able to carry that, will you?'

'We'll have to see about that,' Jodie said defiantly. 'There's a bandage in my first aid kit and I can strap the knee up. That should do the trick. We don't have much choice, do we?'

Maddie knew just how tough and resilient Jodie was and conceded she might even be able to carry her pack too. But it would be a snail's pace for certain and she wasn't sure how far she could travel before aggravating the injury. Surely Jodie couldn't walk the six miles to Bodmin?

But there was another problem too. They now realised they couldn't see the treeline behind them, that's if it was *behind* them, and they couldn't be sure which was the right way to the path. The melee with the sheep had completely disorientated them. Then for some reason, Jodie wasn't sure why, but she checked both her rear pockets before a look of horror spread over her face.

'Shit! My phones gone. I've lost my phone!'

'It must have fallen out back there when you fell over,' Maddie said, wherever *back there* was. Every direction looked the same!

For a moment they stood silent, Jodie wearing a semi shocked expression on her face, looking futilely around at the thick mist before Maddie gasped and snatched her own phone from her pocket.

'I can ring it!' she exclaimed.

Jodie sighed with relief.

It seemed to take ages to change from 'dialling' to 'connected'; a very long time, and Maddie half expected the two little bars to disappear with a 'no signal' message, and for one anxious moment, she wondered if Jodie's phone was switched off and was just about to ask when both girls heard Maddie's phone dialling out.

'Yes!' Maddie said triumphantly.

Then out of the mist came the familiar sound of the Beatles singing, 'It's a hard day's night...' Jodie's chosen ringtone, but it sounded entirely alien now like it didn't belong here, any more than a fish out of water would.

'Gotcha!' Maddie said, homing in on it and looking like she was stalking an escaped chicken back on Jodie's farm. The phone was face down in the grass, glowing bright green around its edges every time it rang. If there had been no mist and it was dark now, Maddie thought she could have spotted it a mile away as it flashed like a beacon.

'Thank god for that,' Jodie murmured when Maddie handed it over. 'Thanks. Don't know why I didn't think of that?'

She held it close in both hands like it was some precious family heir loom she'd lost and just found again.

'You'd better be on your guard,' Maddie said. 'You know what they say about bad things coming

161

in threes?'

'Ha ha, first my leg and then my phone. Wonder what's next?'

'I dread to think.'

Their relief at finding her phone was short lived when they remembered they didn't have a clue which direction the path lay. The only way to find out was to start walking and if they reached the treeline again they knew the path lay directly behind them, or they might just get lucky and hit the path anyway. Of course, there were two other directions to choose from which would almost certainly get them lost. The fact they were standing on level ground didn't help either. If the treeline had been uphill or on a downward slope they would only have two choices. The odds were stacked against them, Maddie thought. A one in two chance was better than one in four any day.

They looked at each other blankly until Maddie broke the silence. 'Which way?'

'God knows. It all looks the same to me'

'Ennie, meenie, miney, mo...' Maddie started to rhyme.

Jodie smiled thinly. 'It might as well be.' She turned to her left. 'How about this way?'

'Why not. It's pot luck now.'

The pace was slow, much slower than before, partly because of the mist but mostly because Jodie couldn't go more than ten minutes without having to stop for a moment and rest her knee. Maddie had visions of Jodie's leg suddenly giving way and she kept close to her the whole time. She didn't want her crumpling to the ground again and making the injury any worse than it already was.

They both recalled it had only taken ten minutes or so to get from the path to the treeline (of course they were moving at half that speed now) and knew if they found nothing in about twenty minutes then they'd chosen the wrong direction and were probably lost. Jodie hadn't brought a compass. It wasn't that she'd forgotten it; just that it hadn't been high on her list of priorities. They were following a trail after all. Now she was regretting her earlier complacency. If she'd had a compass when they'd set off from the path to the outcrop of trees she could have taken a bearing and it would have been easy to find their way back to the path.

After thirty minute's they found neither the path, or any path come to that, or the treeline they'd sheltered under earlier. They had reached an outcrop of rocks and decided it would be a good place to rest for five minutes before deciding their next course of action. The two girls began to feel a little anxious. The mist was showing no sign of lifting; if anything, it looked just as thick as it had been hours before. They checked the time. It was three-fifty pm.

For the time being, they decided to keep going. Both girls were aware that the mist could lift at any time and they still had the map to guide them off the moor. There was also the chance they might come across a prominent landmark, a house or even a farm, anything that might be checkable on the map and give them the bearing they needed to help them get back on track again. Although Jodie had knocked her knee and it appeared to be badly bruised, they weren't in any immediate danger and neither girl wanted to worry their parents. This wasn't the outback where you could easily disappear amongst the hundreds of thousands of square miles of deserts and barren landscape, perhaps even dying from sunstroke, heat exhaustion or dehydration. They still had a bottle of water between them and a couple of bars of chocolate, and they would get through the hunger pangs, get through the discomfort. They weren't at deaths door. Besides, they might have found their way out by the time they were due to be picked up the day after tomorrow and nobody need be any the wiser.

Both girls were sure of one thing; they had youth and resilience on their side and they knew deep down it would only be a matter of time before they found a way out of here.

TEN

If the farmer hadn't come along when he did he might still have them in his sights, Ben thought, but they couldn't be that far ahead of him; surely only a matter of minutes and he'd soon catch up with them if he got a move on. He wondered why they hadn't kept to the trail that would have taken them straight to Bodmin, unless they'd wanted to save some time as there was nothing of any interest whichever route they took. But, they wouldn't get to Bodmin, would they? Not if he could help it. They'd really made it easier for him now though, isolating themselves on the moor by leaving the safety of the trail where most people tended to keep to. And they'd have to separate some time, and when they did he'd be ready to pounce, like a lion stalking a gazelle, waiting patiently for it to stray from the safety of the herd which they always did, eventually.

But he had to ask himself; what if they didn't? They'd stuck together like glue so far and if he was going to fulfil his little plan he had to act on it before they reached the safety of the town they were heading for. He might have no choice but to take both of them on after all, but if he was going to do that he'd need to surprise the bigger girl first. Get her alone. The knife would take care of her. And as for Blondie? Well – once she'd witnessed how he'd dealt with her friend she'd be so scared for her own life she'd be like putty in his hands. She'd do anything he wanted. Now that might work, he thought, unless she reacted differently and ran off into the mist instead screaming her lungs out. That could be messy and he'd never find her again having lost the element of surprise. No - he didn't want her doing that, especially if they were other people nearby who might be alerted by the commotion and come running to her rescue.

He'd have to knock her out first or gag the bitch, before doing away with her; just like he'd done to the last one. Yeah, the last one, remember Benny, that voice in his head

166

reminded him again, and already he could feel the faint beginnings of a headache threatening to make itself at home again.

Ben had found her on one of those adult chat rooms on the internet. Now, wasn't technology a wonderful tool, depending on how you used it of course, allowing him to hide behind a computer screen in a way that a face to face encounter might reveal all sorts of gut instincts and set the old alarm bells ringing in their ears. She'd drop him like a hot potato well before he could get her on her own and away from the safety of prying eyes. She'd been dead easy to reel in though. He knew once he'd told her he had his own cottage in the South West and he lived all by himself on the outskirts of a quaint little village and how his dear old mother had passed away years ago, she'd take the bait like a worm wriggling on the end of a fishing hook. He'd told her he had his own business – a bit if a white lie – but he did work for himself, didn't he? so surely that made it his business. It had worked like a charm though, and the sad part was – not that he had any empathy – that despite the repeated warnings about dodgy internet dating sites or chat rooms, the stupid cows still fell for it, didn't they? But he knew what they'd be thinking. That sort of thing only happens to other people; not me, making Ben think thank god for complacency and the stupidity of women. Not like him though. Although technology was great and all it left a trail behind that could later prove incriminating. But he was smarter than that which is why he always used a false identity and one of those proxy websites that could hide his computers IP address making it look like he was located in a completely different country altogether. He could be in Canada, the Outer Hebrides or Timbuctoo for all they bloody knew. But, it also helped big time if she was keen to hide her own movements, her own identity. Perhaps she was married and wanted a bit on the side or maybe she had some sexual deviance she wanted kept secret from her family, friends and co-workers. And that was exactly the kind of person he was looking for. Someone who had no family, no ties, someone that could easily be overlooked for more than a few hours before the police would be alerted, someone who kept their private lives to themselves and would be reluctant to tell anyone where they were going or what they were doing. Because they had their own little secret. A skeleton in the cupboard, a skeleton he could exploit.

It took a while, trawling the sites for the

right one and then when he saw Mistress Delight or whatever it was she called herself, he thought he might just have hit the bloody jackpot after spending weeks getting nowhere. Profile looked promising: smart 45-year-old single lady. Brunette, five foot six with curves in all the right places. Perhaps a little too curvaceous for his liking judging by the photo, but what the hell. Beggars couldn't be choosers. Looking for some fun. Likes to take control but doesn't mind being dominated by the right man. Likes to be in control, does she? Well, he'd let her do that alright, until it was his turn and then he'd show her what it really meant to be in control.

For over a month they chatted almost daily until she trusted him completely and he sensed she was comfortable with him to the point where he could move it up a notch and suggest they meet up in person. So, when she said she might be able to get away at the weekend and could he pick her up at the train station he thought, bingo! and almost bust his sides laughing at how dumb the bitch was. No one would unduly worry about her if she disappeared for a while. She was divorced three years ago, no kids either. Anyway, hundreds of people went missing every year and just because they did it didn't mean a crime had been committed, did it? Unless they turned up dead somewhere. Some people just wanted to disappear and for any number of reasons. Maybe they were heavily in debt or wanted to escape a marriage that had died a death years ago. Perhaps they'd met someone else and rather than face up to their partner's wrath they just decided it would be far easier just to do a runner.

Everything went great at first. He picked her up in his van and took her back to his cottage without anyone seeing them. It was lucky he didn't live in the middle of the village where everyone knew everyone else's business, or made it their business to find out. The curtains would be twitching before they'd even got out of the van, let alone into the privacy of his cosy little cottage. That was the only trouble living in a shitty little village, living in a rural community that many city dwellers would give their high teeth for. Well, there're welcome to it. Everyone knew everyone else's business and if there was something they didn't know about you, they'd keep probing away until they found out. Why couldn't they mind they own damn business?

So, to avoid the nosy neighbours or curtain twitchers, he preferred to call them, he spun her some cock and bull story about having to work all day – it was a really important job and his client was paying a fortune – he asked her if she wouldn't mind getting a late train and he could pick her up any time after seven pm. Should be dark by the time he brought her home. He'd already checked the train times online and knew that one was due in at seven thirty from Exeter, which was where she was coming from. He nearly split his sides when she told him that was the one she'd catch.

'It's due in at seven thirty,' she'd told him. 'Really?' he'd said. 'That's perfect. I'll be there at seven-thirty, on the dot.'

He'd spent the morning digging some holes for a farmer that needed new fence posts dropping in; hard work but the money was decent enough, reminding him that he'd be finishing after lunch as he had another job to go to. Perhaps spurred on by the anticipation of what was coming later, he worked a little harder than normal and by twelve-thirty he had all the posts in position, much to the delight of the farmer who'd paid him in cash there and then.

That had given him the rest of the afternoon to sort a few things out: a quick trip to the supermarket in Liskeard – seven miles in his van – to grab a case of beer, a couple of packs of cigarettes – he normally rolled his own but *hey this was a special occasion – and a bottle of vodka for her which was the only thing she drank apparently. Well, he hoped she enjoyed it. It had cost him fifteen quid. Not to mention the soda water and lime he had to buy too as that's what she mixed her vodka with. Before leaving the store he grabbed a pizza, thinking to himself he might as well push the boat out. He hoped she appreciated all the trouble he'd gone to. Ah well, he'd told himself, it would be worth it in the end. Spend a little to get a little, wasn't that what they said? Speculate to accumulate, he laughed.*

By eight-thirty the ash tray was half full of cigarette butts and the pair where well on their way. He was on his third can of lager and she must have had four or five vodkas by then. By ten she'd drank half the bottle and he'd had more lager than he'd planned to. Far more. But they were having fun. Everything was going great, until they stumbled into the bedroom. Until he couldn't get an erection, and she started laughing. But her initial amusement soon changed to frustrated anger when she realised that nothing was going to happen in the bedroom department. Not tonight anyway. 'Dickless,' she'd called him. Finishing with a snigger.

She shouldn't have done that, and it was

just the excuse he was looking for. He wiped the smirk away when his fist connected with her drunken face causing her nose to explode with blood running down both cheeks and dripping from her mouth and chin. She wasn't smiling now. The stunned look on her face said it all: 'Did he just punch me in the face?' He'd just stood there, a sarcastic grin on his face, as if to say, what are you going to do about it, eh? But he hadn't expected her reaction – perhaps she'd been battered before and liked to put up a fight (hell she might even enjoy it in some masochistic way) because she flew at him almost immediately after realising he'd broken her nose, clawing at his eyes and screaming like a mad woman. He'd brought up his hands to shield himself but she'd managed to get through with one of her clawed hands and two fingernails gouged deep into his cheek, making his whole face sting like mad. Incensed by the pain, he'd shoved her hard in the chest and she flew backwards onto the bed, the momentum rolling her right over the other side. There was a loud thump and a gasp as she landed hard on the floor.

He didn't have time to assess the damage she'd inflicted; he'd touched his cheek briefly and seen the blood on his fingertips, because she was already regrouping, clutching at the wooden bed post and pulling herself up.

She'd looked like a deranged asylum patient when she managed to stand, with those wide eyes glaring at him through a tangled mess of hair hanging over her blood-soaked face. As she came at him again, her mouth wide open and screaming obscenities, he'd kept his composure, timed it perfectly and thumped her square in the face again, harder this time, fracturing her eye socket and sending her reeling backwards into the bedside locker. He waited for her to get up, half expecting another mad onslaught but she lay motionless on the carpet and it was only when he noticed the blood on the edge of the locker did he know she'd struck the back of her head on the way down. She didn't get back up.

Even though he sensed she was dead as a dodo, Ben went through the motions anyway; checking her pulse and her breathing by putting his ear to her blood-soaked mouth. At one point he thought he'd detected a breath but when the blood oozed from either corner of her mouth, trickling down the sides of her face, followed by a loud wheeze from her lungs had he realised it was only her final breath leaving her body. A death throe. Nothing else. Mistress Delight, or whatever she called herself, had died on him. Cheeky cow. She hadn't even given him the chance to say goodbye – not properly anyway. And he didn't get the chance to torture her either, and that pissed him off more than anything else. He was supposed to be the one in control, not her, and then she'd went and made him do that and took it all away from him. Bloody cow!

Her eyes were open. Dead though she was, he didn't like the way they looked up at him. Like fish eyes they were. Black and staring. He closed them with two fingers so they couldn't accuse him anymore.

He got her corpse into one of those hessian sacks he'd stolen from a barn once – he thought they might come in handy for something – and left it on the bedroom floor until he could dispose of it later, thinking to himself the whole time who was having the last laugh now. The sacks were certainly useful now, he thought to himself. Later, he'd drive out across the moor and find a nice lonely spot to bury the body and provided he dug it deep enough the chances of anybody finding it would be virtually zero. Not out there anyway. It would be like finding a needle in a haystack, or winning the lottery.

And that was the end of that, except it wasn't because he knew it would only be a matter of time before he'd feel the need to kill again, before the compulsion would come back like some annoying itch that could only be relieved by scratching the hell out of it.

He spotted them a few hundred metres along the path in front of him and it looked like they had stopped for some reason. Got you! They were only minutes away. And then the mist came down and it started to rain. Bloody typical, he told himself. But then as he thought about it Ben started laughing to himself – the mist might not be such a bad thing after all – provided he could keep within earshot. He knew this part of the moor better than anybody and there was slim chance of him getting lost, even surrounded by the mist. As well as making things look bigger than they were, the mist had an uncanny ability to amplify sound and that could also work in his favour. Even if he couldn't see them he could certainly hear them, couldn't he? And that really excited him. He could be feet away from them and they wouldn't have a clue, just like the last time when he'd stood there right outside their tent.

Taking advantage of the mist, he hurried along the path, determined to get as close to them as possible. He could be there in no time.

ELEVEN

They walked for another three hours, on and off, and Jodie had slowed considerably as time passed, Maddie insisting they call it a day, concerned that Jodie was pushing herself too much and might cause further damage to her knee. The least it might do would be to slow down the healing process. But that was Jodie all over; stubborn and a bit headstrong at times. But she wasn't stupid either and knew her own limitations, agreeing with Maddie that they should stop soon and find somewhere suitable to settle down for the evening. A complete night's rest could do her knee the power of good.

The mist was still thick, showing no signs of letting up and they came across no houses, farms or any other hapless walkers who might also have gotten lost out here. The moor suddenly seemed a much larger place than how it had looked when they 'd studied it on the computer screen and the map. Most people living here were dotted around its outskirts within easy reach of the roads that would take them away from the moor and into the towns and cities further afield. They hadn't come across anyone and it could only mean one thing. They were heading deeper into the moor itself, in the wrong direction.

They pulled up on a flat area of grassland and took off their packs. It was as good a place as any to pitch their tent for the night and get a good night's rest. With any luck the weather could change overnight and they might wake up in the morning to a bright clear day, the mist a recent memory.

A lone tree stump served as a good spot for Jodie to sit and inspect her aching knee. She untied the bandage and pulled her jeans down below her knees so they could both see her injury. It was red and swollen causing Jodie to wince when Maddie pressed her fingers against the joint. At least it didn't look out of shape which meant it wasn't dislocated, and Jodie still managed to bent her knee with a little pain and some stiffness.

The best treatment, under normal conditions, would have been to rest the limb and apply a cold compress and elevate the leg but these weren't normal conditions, Jodie joking again that she didn't have a bag of frozen peas to hand. Maddie said she could eat a bag of them right now, after thawing them out first, of course. It was ten hours since they'd eaten and they both felt quite hungry now. They broke off three squares of chocolate each and ate them greedily washing it down with a few sips of mineral water which now tasted flat.

Maddie felt the sudden urge to pee. She left Jodie sitting on the tree stump and walked a few feet away, just enough distance to give herself some privacy, unbuckling her jeans as she went. She squatted behind a gorse bush, trying to avoid some reeds that were a little too close, and felt the straw like grass brushing against the side of her bottom, tickling her.

It was then that Maddie first heard the sound, or thought she had as it became drowned out now by the noise of her own urine gushing onto the ground. Finished, she stood up doing up her jeans, and listened. She could hear it now. Running water. There was a stream nearby, and with that revelation came the farmer's voice echoing in her mind. *'Take my advice. If you get lost out here just follow a stream, it'll lead you off the moor; they all do eventually.'* Things seemed to be looking up at last, she thought. They'd had more than their fair share of bad luck recently.

She thought about returning to Jodie first, then decided the stream couldn't be that far away if she could hear it and she might as well have a quick look. She turned, putting her back to the bush and walked towards the sound, travelling no more than a few feet when she spotted the path in front of her. Things were really looking up now, Maddie thought, wondering if by some stroke of luck this could be the same path they'd been looking for all along, but also recognising there were multiple paths on the moor and the chances of it being the one they wanted was probably slim. But paths weren't a design of nature. They were made by humans or the constant traffic of animals and they had to lead somewhere.

Maddie followed the path, the sound of the stream growing louder, and it wasn't too long before she came across a little gully on her right with a gentle flowing stream that disappeared into the mist ahead. Feeling ecstatic now, Maddie couldn't wait to get back to Jodie and tell her the good news, and she realised her friend might be worrying or at least wondering why she was taking so long.

She turned to go back, then noticed something about the path, realising she'd been so preoccupied with the stream she hadn't even noticed how it ended in a fork just feet away. Curiosity got the better of her and Maddie took the left-hand fork in the path, deciding it wouldn't hurt to take a couple more minutes to see where it led. It had to lead somewhere.

Maddie had only taken a few steps when she saw the distinct shape of a figure half hidden by the mist standing on the path in front of her. *Facing her?* Her eyes narrowed against the gloom. Or was the person walking away? She couldn't be sure because the form was just a vague shape and she couldn't discern any noticeable features. But it seemed that her suspicions had been right all along. Others had gotten lost out here and were in the same predicament as they were.

'Hello,' she called, expecting the figure to turn in surprise. To come walking from the mist towards her, perhaps in relief from finding another lost soul. But no response came. The form was perfectly still. *Surely whoever it was must have heard her?*

She moved closer towards the hazy shape, and as the gap closed the figure almost seemed to materialize into something more solid as it broke free from the mist around it.

But Maddie hadn't been prepared for what she now saw. Standing on the path, looking at her was a small girl, and it stopped Maddie dead in her tracks and she could have sworn her heart constricted at the shock just then. The girl was thin, but not painfully so, and looked around ten years old. Blonde hair matched her plain white dress, the hem finishing near her ankles revealing

181

grubby bare feet. There was no expression on the little girl's face, but Maddie sensed a hint of sadness in her eyes as if she had lost something very dear to her.

Suddenly, the little girl breezed right past her catching her by surprise and as Maddie spun around she saw that she was now standing at the fork in the path staring at her again.

Maddie moved closer. 'Please don't be afraid – are you lost?'

The girl giggled mischievously, and taking the right-hand path, disappeared into the mist, leaving Maddie bewildered and a little taken aback at what had just taken place. The first thought that had entered her mind was: poor thing wandering the moor without a thing on her feet and wearing just a dress, but then it *was* the middle of summer and she knew it wasn't uncommon for parents to allow their kids to run around barefoot, especially in rural areas. Hadn't Jodie's parents let them run about barefoot on the farm when she played there as a little girl? Of course they had. The little girl obviously lived around here Maddie decided, and was simply doing what children did: she was out playing. She was playing a little game of hide and seek, that's what she was doing. It did seem odd to her though that her parents would allow their child outside in the misty conditions. But then, she realised the little girl would have been familiar with the local area. Perhaps she lived on a farm close by where they could finally get some help, and she knew she had no choice now but to try and follow her.

Maddie saw the stream running alongside her and wondered how far it travelled before parting company with the path she was now taking. She squinted in the mist but couldn't see the girl yet, but guessed if she was playing a game and wanted her to follow it wouldn't be too long before she couldn't resist showing herself again. She could be hiding anywhere though, Maddie thought, eight or nine feet away enough to render anything or anyone invisible in the thick grey blanket. Including the Beast of Bodmin, it suddenly occurred to her, bringing back thoughts of the conversation they'd had with the farm hand in St Neot and the sound of that fox screaming in the night when she was tucked up in her sleeping bag inside the tent. What was it she'd told Jodie that night? *'If I'd been on the moor in the dark and heard that it would have frightened me to death.'* Well, it's still day time, she told herself, but then realised that the mist more than made up for any lack of darkness and provided little comfort either.

The sound of giggling startled Maddie. She was here. The little girl was right in front of her, hiding just far enough away so that she appeared to Maddie as an indistinct form shrouded by the mist.

She inched forward and Maddie thought right then, if she could just lean forward and stretch out her arm she could probably touch her. But she didn't want to alarm her.

'Hello?' Maddie said softly. 'Do you live around here? I could use some help. Hello?'

And then she was gone again, giggling as she went, and there was no doubt in Maddie's mind now that the mischievous little girl was playing some sort of game with her.

Maddie wasn't sure how much longer she should carry on with this. She really should make her way back to Jodie who was probably worried sick by now. Then it dawned on her. Her phone was in her back pocket all along. She yanked it out and found Jodie's number, her finger hovering over the dial button. She didn't press it; not yet. What would she say exactly? That she had found a path and a stream? Oh, and by the way Jodie I'm playing hide and seek with a little girl I saw barefoot on the moor and I'm following her right now in case she lives nearby and... No, she couldn't tell her all that, not over the phone. It would be like dumping someone by sending them a text message. Way too much to explain and Jodie would think she'd gone nuts. And it was nuts, Maddie thought; maybe she would snap out of it any second now and find herself waking up in her sleeping bag realising it had all been some crazy, confused dream. Except, it wasn't a dream, was it?

Stifled laughter reached her ears. Maddie sighed and slipped her phone back into her pocket. She would give it two more minutes. Then admit defeat.

And then she saw her, just ahead. But the little girl had her back to her now and was walking towards a large dark shape partly obscured by the mist, her white dress flapping around her ankles. Odd! Maddie thought. There was no breeze. Nothing.

At first, she didn't recognise what the shape was until she drew much closer, and then as it appeared in full view, the mist swirling all around it like some ghostly embrace, Maddie caught a fleeting glimpse of white as the little girl disappeared into the house.

But Maddie now saw that this wasn't a normal house. There were no windows or front door and moss clung leech like to most of the slate tiles of the roof. It was merely a stone shell she was looking at, a derelict building that had been abandoned a long long time ago.

At about the same time Maddie was half deciding whether to investigate the house Ben was making his way down the path having already watched her leave the big girl sitting on the tree stump.

The torrential downpour earlier had soaked him to the skin but the warmth to the air had made it more bearable, and in a couple of hours or so he guessed his damp clothes and hair would be dry again. He thought he'd lost them a one stage – when the rain had come – and it was only their garbled voices echoing through the mist that told him they'd left the path and were heading in a different direction, and for a second he wondered if they'd realised someone was following them and were trying to shake him off. It was only when he watched them enter the wood and he crept in amongst the cover of the trees, getting as close as he could to them without being seen – which was a matter of feet – and listened to them talking – although he couldn't pick out every single word – did he realise he was safe, his cover hadn't been blown, and they were merely sheltering from the rain.

He'd shifted position at one point, trying to get as close as possible which was barely within earshot and nothing else. Too close and they were bound to see him. It was right then that the thin branch he'd failed to see cracked under the weight of his foot and he froze, biting his lip and scolding himself for being such an idiot. He stood still, so still that he dared not remove his foot from the branch in *case it creaked in protest. As long as he kept quiet now he should be fine. If he couldn't see them, then vice versa, but he almost died when one of them called out, but he guessed he had it coming to him. Clumsy fool! Ben half expected them to come trampling through the woods hollering again. That would have torn it, wouldn't it? And he'd pulled the knife out, readying himself in case they stumbled across his hiding place. He sensed the danger had passed when they began mumbling amongst themselves again and he carefully took his foot off the branch, relieved when it stayed silent. That was close, too close, he told himself, yet exhilarating all the same, giving him the same kind of head rush he'd felt when he'd smoked some grass recently.*

And he'd kept close to them since; that close at one stage that he'd seen blondie go behind that gorse bush to take a leak and it took a lot of control to stop himself rushing forward then and grabbing her there and then. A hand around her mouth and the knife to her throat; easy as pie. But he wasn't stupid either. She'd have heard him coming for sure and she wasn't out of earshot of her mate. The last thing he needed was butch coming to her rescue with blondie kicking and screaming. He'd never have gotten away with it. Even if

187

she did have a dodgy knee, he laughed to himself, recalling how those bloody sheep had surprised not just them but him also when they came out of the mist like stampeding cattle. It was lucky he'd been behind them at the time and heard the commotion, giving him just enough time to dive for cover. Getting hit by a sixty-kilogram ram at speed was no laughing matter and could do some major damage. Just a shame it hadn't broken her bloody leg though. That would have made things a lot easier for him. She'd been lucky, that's for sure. Even so, the bitch could still move and she'd be on him in no time and it was a risk he wasn't willing to take, not if he could get blondie on her own and well away from her mate.

Tut tut Benny. Now, you wouldn't be afraid of the big girl, would you? It was back in his head again, that damn voice, right inside his brain. You are, aren't you? You're afraid of a woman. Your nothing but a coward. Benny's a coward – afraid of a woman. Ha ha Benny. Your pathetic, you know that!

Oh, you think so do you? Ben retorted. I'll show you what I'm made of, you see if I don't. I'll kill the bitch right now! You just watch me. And then he felt the pain in his head again, but this time it was a thousand times worse, not a throb or a dull ache like the previous headaches he'd experienced but a full-blown stab as if someone had just stuck a knife in his brain and was twisting the blade. He winced, stifling the cry that wanted to burst from his mouth. *Get out! Get out! Get out of my damn head.* And then it was gone, as quickly as it had come, leaving him angry and humiliated that it had laid bare his true fears that festered in the depths of his mind. *I'll show them who's afraid,* he thought, raising the knife in his hand and steeling himself to spring from his hiding place. He'd do it right now; slit her bloody throat and have done with it.

But when he saw her waver, as if something had caught her eye, curiosity held him back and he watched her walk away. In the opposite direction to where her friend was. *Where was she going? Well, whatever it was she was up to she'd just sealed her own fate, that was for certain.* Once she was far enough from her mate back there he'd give a big surprise alright. He just had to be careful to keep his distance and not make any sudden noise. If she got wind of him and ran off into the mist he'd never find her again.

Ben crept out from his hiding place from an even thicker area of gorse and had to admit he wasn't familiar with the path he now stood on, deciding he didn't recognise it because of the heavy mist, but he bet if it suddenly lifted right now he'd know exactly where he was on the moor. But he didn't want it disappearing, not just yet anyway. It had been a god send – the perfect camouflage – allowing him to hide just feet away until the time was right.

He pulled the knife out and flicked open the blade. Step three could be coming up anytime soon and he needed to be ready.

Ben pulled up suddenly when he saw the little girl standing in front of him. He blinked, as if it was a mirage he was looking at and it would fade away if he readjusted his vision. Blinked again. But she was still there, looking right back at him. What the...? What was she doing out here anyway? In the middle of the moor with nothing on her feet. That was all he needed. He'd walked all this way and got soaked to the skin and he wasn't about to let some little brat get in the way of his little plan. She could ruin everything.

Then he heard that voice again, right inside him, but the little girl's lips were moving now as if she were mimicking the words that resonated in his head.

'Hey Benny. You don't mind if I call you that - do you? No, of course you don't.'

Ben flinched, taken back. 'What?'

'We know what you are, don't we Benny? Your one of them, aren't you?'

Ben stumbled forward, shocked by what he was hearing. How did she know to...call him that?

'What you talking about you little brat – what is it that you think you know about me anyway? Huh?'

His fingers tightened round the knife that was down by his side. He wasn't ready to use it just yet; he was curious to know how she knew about him. What she knew about him? And anyway, he didn't feel threatened by a little girl. He didn't need the knife. He could snap her little neck like a twig anytime he wanted.

She grinned, sardonically. 'Oh, I know more than you think Benny. I know you father left when your mother started drinking and then she died from advanced liver cirrhosis when you were thirteen years old, didn't she? And then you went into care until you were...'

'Shut up!' Ben shouted. 'Just shut up, you hear me?'

He edged forward, his grip tightening around the knife. How could she know that? It must be a dream. This couldn't be real and any minute now he'd wake up because that wasn't the sort of thing little girls said, was it?

Her high-pitched tone was that of a child, no doubt – but not the words of innocence, and no little girl had any business talking like that. So, it had to be an illusion, all of it. That voice in his head – it was playing a cruel joke on him. Had to be.

'You're a peeping tom Benny, that's what you are.' she cried.

Ben lunged. 'You what! Come here you little bitch!' But he grabbed only air, surprised by how quickly she'd darted out of the way. Although he hadn't seen how she'd managed to pull that one off. A neat little trick. She hadn't turned and ran. It was like one minute she was here; the next she was over there. In the blink of an eye. But it was no surprise, was it? After all, it was only a dream, and his mind was having a whale of time playing games with him now.

She looked at him smugly.

Ben sneered. 'Think your clever, do you?'

'But your worse than that, aren't you Benny?' the voice said inside as her lips continued to move. 'You're a pervert – nothing but a pervert.'

'Why you little brat!' He lunged at her again, brandishing the knife. 'Come here and I'll show you...' Again, he met empty space and she was feet away once more looking at

192

him and laughing now. Laughing at him and making him angrier.

He brought the knife up level with his face twisting his wrist and showing her the blade. 'You know what I'm going to do. I'm going to cut you up you little cow.'

'You'll have to catch me first Benny.'

'And if you don't stop calling me that,' he said clenching his teeth and shaking his head. 'I swear to god I'm going to kill you right now.'

'Ha ha. You're just a sicko, that's what you are. And what's more, your nothing but a bully.'

Ben just scowled. Keep on talking. That's it, you keep on pushing, he thought, steeling himself for what he knew was coming next. He was going to shut her up. Permanently.

'You're a coward Benny, with a dirty little secret and you're sick in the head, that's what you are,' she mocked. 'But don't worry, your secrets safe with me.'

When she started giggling Ben marched towards her, the knife held straight out in front of him. That was it. She was going to regret it now. Dream, nightmare, whatever it was, he was going to put an end to it right now.

As she disappeared down the left-hand fork he hollered: 'Just you wait till I catch up with you! And I will, you'll see. I'll show you.

I'm going to bloody well kill you.'

Her voice echoed from the mist. 'You mean you're going to murder me Benny – like you did the other poor soul?'

The revelation horrified him, almost sucking the very breath from his soul. Ben whirled around, searching for any sign of her in the mist, but she was nowhere to be seen. How in god's name did she know about that? And then he felt panic. If he didn't find this little brat soon then it would only be a matter of time before his secret was out and they'd come knocking on his door. The only think you're going to be looking forward to Benny, the voice in his head teased, is a very long stretch in some stinking prison cell. Isn't that right Benny? And you'll be rotting in there until your last breath. They don't like being banged up with your sort either. Sickos and perverts are just as bad as child molesters and rapists in their eyes. And once they find out what you're in for – well, it'll be game over for you Benny. You do know that, don't you? If you thought you had it hard at school you haven't seen anything yet. You're in for the shock of your life Benny boy.

But that's not going to happen, the normal voice reassured him, because none of this is real. It's just a nasty cruel trick being played on you by that other voice in your head, the one you shouldn't listen to.

Suppressing the headache he could already feel threatening to invade his skull again, he crept forward along the path, the grip on the knife tightening as his knuckles turned white. He was going to find her, and he'd make her pay. He'd damn well make sure she did.

It started raining again and Maddie decided it was time she headed back. She retraced her footsteps, passing the right-hand fork where she had first seen the little girl, soon reaching the gorse bush she had went behind earlier. She half expected to see Jodie pacing the ground with a concerned look on her face and then grumble to her where she'd been all this time. But there was none of that. Jodie was still sitting on the tree stump and merely gave her a cursory glance as she approached. It was as if she had only been gone a few minutes. But it had to be longer than that. Surely?

'You okay Jodie?'

'Uh-huh,' she said, massaging her knee gently with both hands. 'Here comes the rain again.'

'Yeah, what a bummer. Thought it might have stayed away for a while.' And it was then that Maddie thought she must be going crazy after all, and she seriously considered pinching herself to see if she'd wake up.

'Wasn't too long, was I?' she asked innocently, pulling out a half empty bottle of mineral water from her pack and looking at the contents in disdain.

Jodie screwed her face up. 'Too long? That's a strange question.' She shrugged. 'Four, five minutes, why?'

'Just wondered, that's all.' I *am* going crazy after all, Maddie thought. Four or five minutes? Christ – she must have been gone at least fifteen. What was happening to her?

Jodie was reapplying the bandage to her knee. 'Well, I think we'd better get the tent up before it chucks it down again.'

'Uh?'

'Get the tent up before it rains again.'

'Oh – right.' Maddie tucked the bottle back into a side pouch.

'You okay? Not coming down with something, are you? she inquired, rolling down her trouser leg.

'I'm fine. It's just that...'

'Yes?'

Should she tell Jodie everything? There was a house over there where they could shelter from the rain, wasn't there? But what if she was going crazy? What if she took Jodie all the way down that path and there was nothing at the end of it? No house, maybe even no path, come to think of it. Not only would Jodie think she had completely lost her mind but she would have her own fears rudely confirmed.

And then she blurted it out. 'I think I saw a path back there...'

'A path?'

'...over there behind those gorse bushes. It might not be the same one of course but...'

Jodie's face brightened. 'Well that's good news, isn't it? Why didn't you tell me before?'

'I haven't checked it out yet and I didn't want you getting your hopes up to be honest. I know what you're like Jodie. Your supposed to be resting your leg, aren't you?'

'I'm fine Maddie. But if there is a path over there I'd like to find out. Wouldn't you?'

'What about your knee? You really ought to rest it for a while,' Maddie implored, feeling slightly anxious. Despite her earlier fears, she couldn't understand why she had blurted it out.

Jodie was already hobbling to her feet. 'It'll be okay. I've walked this far, a little more won't hurt. Besides, if that path leads somewhere important we don't want to be sitting here all night, do we?'

'This is exactly why I didn't want to tell you,' Maddie berated her. 'Wish I hadn't now. Your as stubborn as they come.'

Jodie knew Maddie only had her best interests at heart. 'That's true. But it's my leg and it feels fine, honestly. Anyway, for all we know there might be a farmhouse or something down there. Isn't it worth taking a quick look?'

Realising there was no dissuading her now Maddie could only sigh. 'Okay then, if you're sure. But if we find nothing in twenty minutes or so we're coming right back here and putting the tent up. Agreed?'

'I promise,' Jodie said putting her hand over her heart. 'Girl Guides honour.'

TWELVE

But they didn't have to go back and there was no need to get the tent up. The path was real enough and so was the house, exactly where Maddie had seen it, except she didn't let on to her friend that she'd come across it already, nor did she mention the little girl she'd seen running around barefoot on the moor.

She had feigned surprise when Jodie spotted the house, even going so far as telling her it was lucky Jodie had insisted on checking out the path. At least she knew now that she hadn't imagined it so she wasn't going crazy after all, except for the missing time. Now, that was the perplexing part. Perhaps she'd over estimated how long she'd been away from Jodie after all, or maybe Jodie had been so preoccupied herself that it *seemed* she'd been gone for only four or five minutes. And the little girl? Well, as she'd originally thought when she'd first seen her, she must have lived somewhere nearby and was simply out playing. She was probably at home right now, tucked up in bed fast asleep. So why shouldn't she tell Jodie? she asked herself, but deep down she already knew the answer to that one, even though the logical part of her mind had given her the plausible explanation. And yet a doubt remained. There was something odd about it, something that didn't feel quite right and she needed more time to mull it over in her mind before sharing the experience with her friend.

Anyway, there was a more pressing concern right now. The rain was getting heavier and they needed to get to shelter. At least the roof looked surprisingly intact, she saw, even though it was missing its windows and door, as it loomed before them now looking very dark and foreboding engulfed by the mist, and the only thing missing, Maddie imagined, was a streak of lightning and a loud clap of thunder that would complete the eerie scene.

They hurried inside, glad to escape the rain pelting down now just beyond the doorway that once served as a yard or perhaps the front garden. There was nothing inside that gave a clue to its history or the people that once lived there. It was just a stone shell, home now to the weeds that grew unhindered between cracks in the stone floor and perhaps the occasional rat or mouse that happened across it in search of food or shelter. The thought that rodents might be lurking in the dark cracks and crevices of the house made Maddie shudder, and if she hadn't been tired, hungry and wet, she would have gladly given the house a miss and opted for the tent instead.

Maddie sat down wearily, resting against the rough stone wall in the largest room that had probably been the main heart of the house, listening to her stomach grumbling in protest that it hadn't had a meal in over ten hours. She wondered idly about the people that once lived here. It had probably been a farmhouse at one time; it seemed too large to have served as a family home and if her memory of Cornish history was correct many folk back then would have farmed these moors or mined the copper and tin mines.

Her pack was next to her. She opened a side pouch and took out what was left of the chocolate bar. She slowly unwrapped the paper and foil, too slowly almost, as if it was a birthday present she'd been given and wanted to savour the moment. She half hoped to see more than she expected. A nice little surprise. *You haven't eaten as much as you thought Maddie. There's half a bar here.* But there were only four squares. She broke off two and nibbled on them fighting the urge to wolf them down.

Her head started to itch and she scratched her scalp. The relief was only temporary when she felt the itchiness on a different part of her head and she scratched at it again, vigorously this time. She sniffed under her armpit like she had done that morning after waking in the tent. This time the smell was pungent. Not to the point of making her want to retch. After all, this wasn't a foreign body. This was *her* body. *Her* smell. Even so. Yuck! She wrinkled up her nose, quickly dropping her arm.

'Pigs don't smell their own shit.' Jodie had said. Well, this time she begged to differ. Today, this little piggy had a keen sense of smell.

Inspecting her fingernails, she saw they were dirty. Embedded under her nails like she had raked the bare earth with her hands. Maddie longed for a shower. To be clean again. She knew then, although she wouldn't admit it to Jodie, this wasn't for her: the grime, the sweat, the discomfort of getting wet to the skin and the itchiness that never went away. Especially the itchiness. And the smell!

Images formed of the 'down and outs' she had seen sleeping rough in the city. Some of them looked like they hadn't bathed in a month, judging by the soiled clothes, the way their matted and greasy hair clung to their face and the whiff she'd sometimes got when she walked past. The stench was the worst. A mixture of stale sweat and urine. Except this time, she was the one in the doorway, huddled beneath a grimy blanket or under a piece of cardboard. And she was the one being given a wide berth or a startled look from passers-by as she held out her trembling grubby hand for a few coins. She was the one who *stank* to high heaven.

'Hey lady! You could do with a bath,' jeered a group of lads returning from the pub.

'Stinking bitch!' Laughing and grumbling amongst themselves as they walked off that the authorities shouldn't allow it. They shouldn't have to see it and *her* kind shouldn't be allowed on the streets.

Maddie had never held those views. Sadly though, some did. The world seemed a twisted place at times, she thought.

Time ticked by. Slowly.

They cleared an area of loose stones and rubble before laying down their bed rolls and sleeping bags. Maddie got into hers and lay there in the semi darkness listening to the nothingness. Just that pleasant buzzing in her ears again. Silence was indeed golden and she knew what it meant now. Tiredness crept over her and she chose not to fight it, letting her eye lids close as she drifted quietly towards sleep.

As it grew dark, a small furry shape peered out from its hiding place beneath a lengthy crack in the floor, brushing past Maddie's sleeping bag as it scurried about the room searching for food. Maddie was unaware of its presence as she moved deeper towards the dream state, images beginning to stir in her mind, memories from her conscious and sub conscious all jumbled up making the experience fragmented and nonsensical as most dreams seemed to be.

She was on the path again, the little girl standing there and looking at her with the same sad expression on her face. Maddie saw she was painfully thin, as if she hadn't eaten in weeks, her white dress now a dirty grey and her skin pallid. Dark shadows encroached around her sunken eyes that seemed to have lost their sparkle and a blue tinge to her lips and cheeks made it look like she was suffering from the cold. Grubby feet protruded below the hem of her dress but the toe nails had now turned black. She breezed past Maddie again and was standing at the fork in the path, a blackened finger nail pointing in the direction of the house. Maddie opened her mouth to speak, but nothing came out, and the little girl stepped forward and disappeared into the mist. Maddie tried to follow but she couldn't move her legs. She tried hard to lift her feet but they were stuck fast, as if they were encased in concrete. And then everything around her faded away.

She was on the train again, watching the old lady knitting with gnarled sinewy fingers except now some of the flesh had peeled away revealing the white bone beneath and her fingernails were so black it looked like they had died. And when Maddie looked up she saw an old hag sitting there, tufts of white hair hanging from her balding head, and black eyes sunken beneath taut skin that it made her think it was a living skull she was looking at. A stench assailed her nostrils, something very unpleasant like the smell meat made when it was starting to go bad. It was the smell of rotting flesh.

The old hag leaned close, and Maddie retched from the rancid smell on her breath. 'Before you know it, a mist can come down in no time,' she cackled, cracked lips revealing rotting gapped teeth and Maddie recoiled in horror turning to flee from the nightmarish vision.

She was running now, as fast she could and yet she couldn't escape because everything seemed to slow down and she sensed that thing was right behind her the whole time, whispering close to her ear. 'Take care now dear, the both of you...' And then she

205

was gone, her voice fading away to the faint sound of horse's hooves pounding the earth, growing louder and louder until the black horse and carriage pulled up abruptly.

It was outside the house, the one she now sheltered in, waiting for her. Waiting for her to come out. But she didn't want to. Yet, despite her fear, she found herself going out there anyway, as if she was part of some weird screwed up movie that was being played out in front of her over which she had no control.

'Come on up…missy,' a voice said, and as she climbed up a bony hand extended towards her. Looking up at his face she saw strands of white hair protruding from his tricorne hat but the face had gone now, replaced by a skull grinning down at her with eyeballs moving in their sockets, its jaw opening and closing and repeating the words 'come on up…missy'. It reminded her of a macabre ventriloquist's dummy that had taken on a life of its own and Maddie couldn't hear her own screams; her mouth was wide open but no sound reached her ears… Then the skull was shouting, 'Maddie!… Maddie!'

'Maddie! – wake up,' Jodie said, shaking her shoulder. 'Maddie!'

Her eyes snapped open and she was staring

into semi-darkness, a familiar figure standing over her. She slumped forward, relieved that it wasn't real, that the nightmare was over and trying to make sense of it all while it was still fresh in her mind.

'You okay Maddie?'

'Ugh?' she gasped, putting her hands in her face as a deep breath whooshed from her lungs. 'Christ...that was awful.'

'You scared the life out of me. Looked like you were having a bad dream.'

'A nightmare,' she corrected her. 'A horrible nightmare.' She sighed heavily, realising the last time she'd had a nightmare this bad was when she was about eleven years old, but it hadn't been anywhere near as graphic as this one. The years had dulled her memory now but it had been something to do with little people or trolls that were all around her, closing in on her as she lay helpless in her bed, paralysed with fear, creeping towards her with their arms extended like zombies and getting closer and closer. She had woken up just as they were about to touch her, she remembered.

'What time is it?' Maddie asked groggily, forgetting the watch on her wrist. It took a few seconds to readjust to her surroundings.

'Just after seven.' Jodie sat down beside her. 'I didn't know you had nightmares.'

'I don't,' she said flatly. 'Not since I was a kid anyway.'

'You were talking in your sleep too.'

'Was I?

'Yes, and loud enough to wake the dead too. You were muttering something or other but I couldn't make it out. A load of gibberish, if you ask me. When you started screaming I thought I'd better bring you out of, and quick.'

'Glad you did. Sorry if I woke you.'

'Oh, don't worry about that,' she said. 'What I'd like to know, is what you were dreaming about? You do realise you nearly gave me a heart attack?'

'Did I? Well, I didn't do it on purpose,' Maddie managed to smile now.

'So – you going to tell me or not?'

Maddie recounted her nightmare but decided not to mention the little girl, partly because she knew she would feel compelled to reveal the secret she had kept about her appearance on the path – the old lady on the train and the dark horse and carriage events that Jodie already knew about – but because she was reluctant to face up to her own mounting fears that were growing in her mind but which she hadn't yet fully understood.

Jodie wondered if hunger, the dank atmosphere of their surroundings, not to mention talk of the Bodmin Beast and that grisly story she'd told her in the tent the other night had somehow

208

played a part in contributing to her nightmare, and she had listened quietly while Maddie had recounted it. Finally, she spoke. 'I think that definitely falls into the nightmare category. Sounds like something right out of a Stephen King novel.'

'Well, I've never read any of his books and if they're as bad as that nightmare, I don't think I'll be borrowing them from the library any time soon.'

'Do they even stock those sorts of books in the university library?'

Maddie shook her head. 'No, not really. Not the same as public libraries do, but we do have some fiction on the shelves, but it's more likely to be books that support students studying English literature for example. You won't find the popular romance or crime novels sharing space with Shakespeare or Chaucer,' she managed to laugh now. 'And I don't think horror would get a look in either.'

Jodie raised her eyebrows. 'I suppose not,' she conceded. 'I hadn't really thought about it like that to be honest.'

Before Jodie had time to ponder the answer, Maddie asked, 'Do you think dreams or nightmares have some sort of hidden meaning?'

The sudden question caught Jodie by surprise and it took her a moment to collect her thoughts.

'I'm no expert, but I've got one of those books at home. A to Z of dream interpretations I think it's called, but I could never understand any of it quite frankly. It recommends you keep a notebook and pen by your bed and if you have a dream you should write it down before you forget all about it.'

'That makes sense,' Maddie said. 'By the time I'm out of bed its gone in an instant.'

Maddie had seen those sorts of books on the shelves in Plymouth and she was sure she'd overlooked one in one of the bargain bins she liked to rummage through now and again. But the subject had never interested her enough to want to buy one. Most of the time she couldn't remember her dreams anyway and assumed they were just a mixed jumble of memories played by her mind.

'From what I can gather,' Jodie said. 'Dreams are supposed to be symbolic and not to be taken literally. Something to do with the way the sub conscious mind interprets things.'

'You mean like the one where you dream about your teeth falling out but it's really supposed to mean someone in your family or someone close to you is going to die soon?' Maddie remembered reading that in a magazine.

'Exactly. But how they can know that's what it *really* means is beyond me,' Jodie said. 'As for your dream, nightmare or whatever you want to call it – well – god only knows how to interpret that one.'

'I dread to think,' Maddie shuddered. 'I wouldn't know where to start.'

Something had caught Jodie's attention just then, because she got up from the floor and crossed to the doorway. She stood there for a moment, peering out.

'I think you'd better take a look at this?'

'What is it?'

Maddie guessed the rain had eased because she could barely hear it now. Scrambling to her feet she joined her friend at the doorway. 'Stopped raining at last, has it? she asked.

The doorway was narrow and Jodie had to angle herself to allow Maddie some space.

'Yes, but not just that,' she indicated with her head. 'See for yourself. It could be my imagination but it looks like the mist is lifting.'

Maddie peered out curiously, suppressing any hint of premature excitement. She wanted to be sure but it didn't take too long for the smile to spread all over her face. 'It looks like it, doesn't it? About time too.'

Stepping outside and taking everything in, both girls realised that it wasn't so gloomy any more, the mist unveiling increasingly more of the landscape and it's features as it receded away from them, back across the moor.

And something else had revealed itself too they noticed, and they ran across until they were standing beside it.

Maddie wasn't sure which to be more thrilled

about first: the trail she was now standing on or the welcoming sign she looked up to: 'JAMAICA INN 4 MILES.'

Both girls regarded each other in stunned silence. They'd spent all night in that house, oblivious to the fact there was a trail no more than twenty feet away and an inn just a few short miles down the trail. It was then that the pair of them broke into fits of laughter.

THIRTEEN

The knife was by his side, like a sheriff holding his six shooter in front of him in one of those old western movies as he walked down the street scanning the rooftops and buildings for the bad guys that might appear at any moment. With each deliberate step he'd half turn right and left, as if expecting her to suddenly appear from the mist and catch him by surprise. But he was the one doing the stalking, wasn't he? And that's exactly what it felt like to him. He was the hunter and she was the hunted. Ben was the sheriff and she was the baddie. Another vision unfolded in his mind, making him chuckle inside. He was Sylvester and she was the cat. She was the puddy tat, and the cartoon song began playing in his head.

I am a little tiny bird. My name is Tweety Pie. I live inside my bird cage, a hanging way up high. I like to swing upon my perch and sing my little song but there's a tat that's after me and won't let me alone.

I taut I taw a puddy tat a creepin' up on me. I did! I taw a puddy tat as plain as he could be!

I am that great big bad old cat, Sylvester is my name. I only have one aim in life and that is very plain. I want to catch that little bird and eat him right away, but just as I get close to him, this is what he'll say.

I taut I taw a puddy tat a creepin' up on me. You bet he taw a puddy tat, that puddy tat is me!

That puddy tat is very bad, he sneaks up from behind. I don't think I would like it if I knew what was on his mind. I have a strong suspicion that his plans for me aren't good. I am inclined to think that he would eat me if he could.

I'd like to eat that tweetie pie when he

leaves his cage. But I can never catch him, it throws me in a rage. You bet I'd eat that little bird if I could just get near. But every time that I approach this is all I hear.

I taut I taw a puddy cat a creepin' up on me. I did! I taw a puddy cat as plain she he could be!

And when I sing that little song, my mistress knows he's back. She grabs her broom and brings it down upon Sylvester's back.

So listen you bad puddy tat, lets both be friends and see. My mistress will not chase you if you sing this song with me.

I tau I taw a puddy cat a creepin' up on me. I did! I taw a puddy cat as plain she he could be!

Sudden laughter startled him and the vision vanished from his mind. Ben froze, unsure which direction it had come from. In front of him or behind? Or maybe away from the path, either side of him on the grass. Trying to trick him, trying to sneak up on him. Ben couldn't pin point the exact direction. It seemed like it had come from – well – all *around him…*

'Come out, come out, wherever you are,' he taunted. 'I know you're here.' The whites of his eyes were the first thing you saw, so wide were they.

Then he heard a giggle. Right in front of him. Playing games with him, was she? She wouldn't be laughing in a minute, not when he found her and got her by her scrawny little neck. Then he'd shut her up for good. Just like Sylvester would, when he caught the tweety pie…

I taut I taw a puddy tat a creepin' up on me…

Suddenly she was in front of him, partly shrouded in the mist but she had her back to him this time. Got you now, you little brat, he thought, creeping forward, realising if she'd known he was behind her she'd have turned around by now. She was about to get a nasty surprise. He'd slit her bloody throat!

He got to within reaching distance and stretched out his hand intending to grab a handful of hair or the back of her dress near the neck. Once he'd got hold of her she wasn't going anywhere. But as his fingers clawed at the top of her dress he felt nothing but air as his hand passed straight through her, as if she was some sort of hologram. He staggered back and his knees went weak. What the...?

She turned and faced him, laughing as she did and Ben recoiled in shock when he saw the coal black eyes staring into him. Her face was as white as bleach and her cheeks and lips tinged frosty blue like she had spent some time trapped in one of those walk-in freezers. She didn't look very well at all, like one of the undead from those cult zombie films he liked to watch. Even the white dress looked filthy now and as he looked down to her grubby feet he saw her toenails had turned black. Her hair no longer shone but looked dry and brittle, hanging from her scalp in thin strands, like some terminally ill patient dying from a radiation overdose.

Ben froze. But this couldn't be real – it had to be some sort of nightmare and any second now he'd wake up in the sanctuary of his little cottage near the village. But he guessed it was his own fault for watching too many of those zombie movies, his overactive imagination now coming back to haunt him.

As if to dismiss the vision before him he closed his eyes tight, but a voice spoke to him before he could open them again.

'You can't murder me Benny. You know

that, don't you?'

His eyes snapped open. She was still there. 'Uh – what?'

'You can't kill me Benny. It's much too late for that,' she giggled, and this time he caught a glimpse of some black rotting teeth.

Ben stood his ground, but was wary of advancing any closer. 'What are you talking about? You're not real, are you? I know you're not. It's that voice inside my head again...'

'You can't murder me because I'm already dead,' she screeched with laughter. 'Haven't you realised that yet Benny?'

Ben's head spun, and he felt a sharp pain near his temple, as if someone had poked something sharp in there. She'd better stop calling him that. Benny this, Benny that, just like his damn mother used to. Just like the other kids at school did when they taunted him like that, calling him names. It was all her fault. That bloody cartoon. Top Cat. She said he'd looked like Benny, with that chubby little face of his and those little dark round eyes. Bloody Benny from Top Cat! A cartoon character. It had followed him when he started secondary school and it was different there. The kids were older, a bit savvier and a lot crueller and they'd teased the hell out of him and made his life a misery.

'Hey Benny! how's TC?'

Top Cat was the gang's cool leader – but Benny was anything but cool; the equivalent of the village idiot.

'Ha ha Benny. Seen Officer Dibble lately? How's your mum doing by the way?' Sniggering. 'Mum told my dad she was drunk when she picked you up from school last week.'

'Benny's mums a drunk...Benny's mums a drunk...'

She'd been half cut that day. Everybody had seen her, including the teacher and it wasn't long before Social Services had paid them a little visit. Once or twice he'd gotten into a fight over it all and always came off worst. There were four of them; one of him, and he never stood a chance.

And it had all been her fault...and then she'd driven his father away with her constant drinking sessions and her mood swings. And then, to top it all, she went and died on him, leaving him on his own... Well, I hope she's rotting in hell right now, he thought.

'It's a dream I tell you! You're not real,' he screamed.

'Oh, but I am Benny, and there's someone here who's dying to see you. Excuse the pun, won't you,' she sniggered. 'Someone you

219

haven't seen in a long while, someone who's got a bone to pick with you.' Her finger pointed accusingly at him.

'No! You're just a stupid little brat. You're playing with my head, that's what you're doing. The voice in here!' He tapped his finger on the side of his head. 'Your screwing with my mind.' A grin stretched the corners of his mouth when he realised he had the knife in his hand, and he lifted it up so she could see the point of the blade, raising it over his head and moving towards her.

Like some spectral ghost appearing to Jacob Marley on the stroke of midnight, she raised her arm straight up and pointed over his shoulder. He balked at the blackened fingernail he could now see.

Ben turned, aware now of something or someone that was standing behind him.

His eyes widened. 'You!' he gasped, staggering backwards, the shock making his legs go weak as they quivered beneath him, and for one horrible second he thought his bowels might even open.

'It can't be!' his voice trembled. 'Your…your…'

'…Dead?' the familiar figure rasped, glaring at him.

'No! you can't be!' he screeched this time.

'You weren't breathing I tell you...I buried you good and proper too...how...?

She was six feet away, standing – no! not standing, Ben was horrified to see as he looked down to the bare feet that hung inches above the ground. Impossible though it seemed, the bitch was...she was...floating in the mist!

Ben stood aghast, dimly aware now of the warmth that trickled down his leg as a puddle of his own urine formed around his feet. She was wearing that blood stained white blouse, the short black bulging skirt that threatened to burst the zip at the side and black shiny tights, laddered all the way down one leg and with holes over the knee caps. Her nose had been smashed to a pulp, blood oozed from her lips and trickled down the sides of her face from the fractured and blackened eye sockets above. Desperately, he fought to tear himself away from the hideous spectacle standing before him, but his legs refused to move. It was as if he was being forced to watch, held there by some invisible force and condemned to face the victim of his own brutality. Like some sort of macabre torture, of which he was the victim.

Mistress Delight, or whatever it was she liked to call herself before joining the realm of the dead, floated right up to him. Dumbstruck,

Ben shut his eyes tight as she hovered inches from his face, and his shaking hand, now useless, dropped the knife to the ground.

'You! You murdered me...And now...now you're going to pay...'

Ben screamed in terror, and the force holding him seemed to weaken from his outcry because he could now move his feet. He turned and ran, desperate to escape the horror behind him and blinded by fear he passed through the spectral form of the little girl that was blocking the other direction.

Ben didn't care that in the mist he couldn't see where he was going. He was petrified and had to get away, as quickly and as far from the nightmare as possible. Before it drove him mad.

FOURTEEN

It was a welcome sight when the Inn came into view from across the moor, the grey granite building with its black slate roof looking somewhat foreboding as it dominated the higher ground and Maddie wondered what three-hundred-year-old secrets lay within its walls. It was a tantalising thought.

Maddie had read about Jamaica Inn in the guidebook before they'd left the derelict house. Built in 1750 it had been used as a staging post for changing horses and had welcomed weary travellers crossing the moor for nearly three hundred years. It had also been used as a stopping point by smugglers as they moved their contraband of brandy, rum and tea around the country and it was thought it got its name from the smugglers

223

who had brought rum into the country from Jamaica and stored it at the inn. Credible though it seemed, the inn's name was believed to derive from a local Trelawney family of landowners, two of whom served as Governors of Jamaica in the eighteenth century.

Neither girl had gone so long without food and it was the main topic of conversation, realising now that a hot meal and a drink lay just inside. Like a couple of excited kids on a trip out to McDonalds or Kentucky Fried Chicken, they chittered non-stop, speculating what delights might be on the menu and what they were going to have: steak and kidney pudding, fish and chips, bangers and mash or a roast chicken or beef dinner. It didn't matter which; they all sounded equally as good when you were starving.

Jodie still limped as she walked, but her knee had held up well and didn't seem to be getting any worse, and Maddie knew it would only be a matter of hours before they got out of here and she could have it checked out at the local hospital on the way home. And it wouldn't be too long after that when she could take a nice hot shower or even better a long soak in a bath full of bubbles. Her head itched. It felt like there were hundreds of nits in her hair or some other crawling things that had invaded her scalp overnight. But it was more likely dirt and sweat accrued over the past two days that was the real cause of her discomfort now. That she knew. She couldn't wait to wash away the grime and the unpleasant odour she was now acutely aware of, and just hoped to god other people wouldn't notice it when she got to the inn that was now only minutes away.

The face of a pirate scowled at them. The sign hung from a black wooden post that stood inside the low stone wall that separated Jamaica Inn from the pavement and roadside running the length of its front. He was wearing a black eyepatch – didn't all pirates, Maddie mused – with a colourful parrot on his right shoulder and a half sunken sail ship lying in the bay beyond. The inn might well have appeared frozen in time had it not been for the picnic tables and umbrellas spread out across the cobbled courtyard that catered now for an entirely different kind of visitor.

Standing in the courtyard, Maddie couldn't help but to admire the historic two storey building, with its gabled porch over the front entrance and flanked either side by old fashioned light casements – not dissimilar to the smaller type one might find on a Victorian horse and carriage – perched high on black metal lamp posts. A rusty ships anchor sat proudly to her left and two wooden wagon wheels rested against the walls either side of the main door. A red telephone box to her right looked oddly out of place. There was something surreal about it all, and Maddie could almost feel the mood of intrigue, of something secretive and hidden, perhaps trapped within the very fabric of the building itself that would manifest itself during the hours of darkness, leaving no visitor untouched by the experience after spending a night here alone. She could just imagine what it must look like here on a moonlight night, the sign creaking as it swung in the wind and the inn bathed in the eerie yellow glow from the light casements that overlooked the courtyard. If ever she needed a reason to read the novel Jamaica Inn, this was it, her imagination fired now so that a visit to the library would be inevitable on her return home.

Jodie phoned her mum, telling her there had been a change of plan and could she pick them up from Jamaica Inn instead of St Breward. There was nothing to worry about and she'd tell her everything later.

Deeming it safe to do so, they left their backpacks outside before Maddie pushed open the black door and entered the famous inn.

A few people were having a late breakfast when they went inside and the girls looked on ravenously as they found themselves a table in the corner by the window. They wasted no time in ordering the full English breakfast with extra toast and a pot of coffee for two. When the food arrived, they had to hold themselves back or risk disapproving stares from the other diners, oblivious to the fact the girls hadn't had a proper meal in over thirty hours. When they finished, they ordered more coffee, Maddie remarking she could eat it all over again as they sat back in their seats resting inflated stomachs and taking in their surroundings.

The floor was carpeted a blood red, contrasting nicely with the dark wooden beams running the length of the white plaster ceiling. The room was adorned with all kinds of memorabilia: brass and copper kettles, horse bridles, old bank notes framed under glass, horse brasses on leather straps and black and white photographs on nearly every wall, many depicting the history of the inn itself and the local moorland community it served. The main bar area where they sat had a large granite fireplace and Maddie imagined how cosy it must have been here during the winter months with the logs crackling and fire roaring in the corner. A door led to the Smuggler's Bar with the sign 'Through these portals passed smugglers, wreckers, villains and murderers, but rest easy...t'was many years ago.' There were twenty rooms at the inn, all with on suite and Maddie was surprised to learn that all of them had flat screen televisions with Sky TV Channels and even Wi fi, rivalling some prestigious hotels with five star ratings. For such an historic building it had been kept well up to date with the latest technological amenities, she thought to herself.

Jodie was thumbing through a leaflet she had found. 'Hey – listen to this?'

Maddie was enjoying her third cup of coffee, the caffeine imbuing a tranquil affect that served to lighten her mood and she rested back in her seat now succumbing to the sudden weariness she felt from the previous day's exertions.

'The writer, Daphne du Maurier, got her inspiration for the novel Jamaica Inn – published in 1936 – from the time she had spent here in this very inn. Apparently, she had been out horse riding with a friend when they got lost in the fog and their horses led them back to the safety of the inn.'

'Really? I knew she wrote it but that's about all. We aren't the only ones to have got lost in the mist then?'

'Apparently not,' Jodie continued. 'And we probably won't be the last either. It also says that during the early nineteen hundred's the inn was used as a temperance house, but there have been spirits of a completely different kind at Jamaica Inn. Previous managers and employees have heard talking uttered in a strange foreign tongue and some say the language could be old Cornish.'

'Temperance house?'

'It means they didn't sell alcohol. Religion was behind it, brought about by the temperance society; a group of Methodists who advocated moderation in all things, especially alcohol consumption. They even had their patrons sign a pledge to give up the evil drink completely.'

'How do you know all that?'

'History always was my strong point.'

'Hmmm. You mean you saw it on a documentary somewhere?'

Jodie sniggered. 'Of course I did silly. I couldn't stand history at school; bored me to death, as you well know. Anyway, mum was watching it too and she said she remembered gran saying there had been a temperance bar in the village she lived in.'

'So, the inn is haunted then? You said something about spirits?'

Jodie nodded. 'I'm not surprised given the age of the building and its colourful history. It says here that some guests have reported hearing horses' hooves and the metal rims of wheels turning on the cobbles in the courtyard and footsteps pacing the corridors outside their rooms in the dead of night. Some also claimed to have seen a strange man in a three-cornered hat and cloak who appears and then walks through solid doors.'

'Oh great,' Maddie said, remembering her nightmare. 'If you're trying to frighten me you're doing a good job.'

'You'll like this one then,' Jodie carried on

eagerly. 'Some claimed to have seen an anguished young mother with a baby who inhabits the mirror in room five and a murdered young smuggler who paces around the courtyard in the middle of the night.'

'Oh! that's creepy,' Maddie shuddered, rubbing away the goose bumps that had bristled over her arms.

Jodie grinned. 'It is a bit, isn't it? So, you won't be booking a room here in a hurry then?'

Maddie shook her head. 'Not on my own I wouldn't – would freak me right out. I mean, don't get me wrong or anything – it might be a bit of fun and all but I don't think I'd get any sleep. I'd be lying there all night listening to every bloody creak.'

'Well, there is a story going around about a couple that booked a room here but they didn't survive the night. Packed up their things and left in the middle of the night, so the story goes.'

'Why doesn't that surprise me,' said Maddie.

'I know, but it would be a laugh, wouldn't it? It says some of the guests come here specifically to stay overnight because it's supposed to be haunted – ghost hunters too apparently. And a television crew filmed here a while back for that 'Most Haunted' series with...what's his name...? the medium – Derek Acorah,' she suddenly recalled.

'Rather them than me. Gives me the creeps just

thinking about it. It's probably not so bad in a group, but when they go off exploring on their own in the pitch black with just a night vision camera and a radio...'

'Yeah, I know. You wouldn't get me doing that either; unless they offered me a serious amount of cash.'

Maddie shook her head. 'Nope. Think I'd still chicken out. Moneys not much good if you've given yourself a heart attack.' She got up from her seat, looking around the room. 'Anyway, I need the loo. Way too much coffee. Any idea where it is?'

'Over there,' Jodie said, pointing to a door that Maddie had her back to.

Maddie headed that way, noticing the numerous pictures adorning the wall to her right. Passing through the bar area she saw a bespectacled man wiping down the counter and a woman laying out some beer mats.

'Good Morning,' they greeted her.

Maddie returned the compliment. 'Morning.'

On her return one of the pictures caught her eye and she stopped to look, leaning close to the thin card fixed along the bottom of the frame: 'A typical moor farming family. Circa 1895.' It was a black and white photo of a couple in front of their farmhouse, their daughter standing between them as they posed for the camera. It was difficult to guess how old the husband and wife were, Maddie conceded. Both looked weather beaten, their rugged and tanned complexions testament to the harsh conditions and the spartan lifestyle they would have endured back then. Without the benefit of modern farming equipment, it must have been back breaking work to say the least. Clothed, though they were, there wasn't an extra ounce of fat on their wiry looking frames, contrasting starkly with the appearance of modern people who benefited from automation and an abundance of highly processed foods.

Maddie put the girl at around nine or ten. Her hair was light and Maddie surmised she was probably blonde – a colour photo would have substantiated that – and she was wearing a white dress all the way down to her ankles. When she noticed nothing on her feet and she was barefoot on the grass, Maddie felt a cold shiver down the back of her neck and she began to feel queasy. No – it wasn't possible. How could she even consider it? But she had to admit – the girl in the photo bore an uncanny resemblance to the little girl she had seen on the moor. But it wasn't – was it? The world was full of little coincidences, and this was just one of them.

Then something tugged at her mind again, something that had been gnawing away at her since she'd recalled the old lady's remark: *'Take care now – the both of you.'* Had she misheard her? And it was then that Maddie's eye's fixed on the woman in the photo, the mother with the light-coloured hair standing proudly beside her daughter and Maddie felt a growing sense of disquiet as that same chill come over her again and her head stated to spin at the sudden realisation...

She glanced towards the bar, and saw the man was on his own now and cleaning some glasses. It was early yet and no one was being served. She went over. Looking down to his task, Maddie saw the middle-aged man was balding on top with a smattering of black and grey either side his bulbous looking head, and the round spectacles perched over his small hooked nose made him appear almost owl like. He was dressed casually, wearing a green cardigan buttoned up to a protruding middle over a plain flannel cream shirt. She thought it odd he was wearing a cardigan in the middle of summer.

He looked up from the wine glass he was cleaning, peering at her over the rim of his spectacles. 'Was everything okay with your breakfast?'

'The food was fine thanks. I was just looking at that photo over there.' She pointed it out. 'The family with the farmhouse in the background.'

He leaned across the bar and squinted, before raising his glasses away from his eyes. 'That's better. I'm long sighted you see,' he explained, holding the rim between his finger and thumb. 'Only really need these for close work.'

Maddie just nodded, smiling as she did.

'Now then. The photo. Oh yes – I see the one you mean.' He settled his spectacles back on his nose before turning his attention back to Maddie. 'So how can I help you?'

'Do you know anything about the photo. The family I mean?

'Ah – you want the wife. She's the expert and knows far more about that sort of thing than me.' He leaned close as if he had some secret to impart. 'To be honest, it's a bit of a hobby of hers. Ever since we took over this place nearly ten years ago, she's made it her business to find out as much as she can about the local area and the history of the moor in particular. The visitors we get here are understandably curious about that sort of thing, Jamaica Inn especially with its tales of smugglers and highway men, not to mention the inevitable ghost stories. A three-hundred-year-old building with such a colourful past is bound to have the odd ghost or too. The guests that stay here just love that sort of thing.'

Maddie could empathise with that. 'I'm sure they do, and so would I come to think of it.'

'We've even had people from abroad staying here,' he carried on enthusiastically. 'A couple from America, would you believe. Came all the way over here just so they could spend a week in one of the rooms.'

'Really?' Maddie was genuinely surprised.

'Oh yes. But they were very insistent though. Had to be room five they said. And they were quite prepared to wait until that particular room became available. They made that very clear.'

'Isn't that supposed to be the most haunted room? The lady in the mirror with the baby?'

'That's it yes, along with room four. I see you've been reading up on it then? Thankfully, they weren't disappointed either. They both said they'd experienced something out of the ordinary. If truth be told I think it frightened them half to death because they didn't hang around after checking out either,' he chortled.

'I bet they didn't,' Maddie grinned, looking around the room for any sight of his wife returning.

'Anyway, you don't want to stand around here all day listening to me prattling on, do you?' he said almost apologetically. 'She should be back any minute. I'm certain she can tell you everything you want to know – I'd be surprised if she can't.'

'That's okay. I don't mind waiting.'

'Can I get you anything in the meantime. A drink perhaps?'

Before she could answer the door to the smugglers bar swung open and his wife appeared carrying a tray of empty glasses. In complete contrast to her husband Maddie thought she looked perfectly normal. A tad on the thin side perhaps but not to the point of making her look gaunt. She was wearing a sleeveless white blouse, complimented by a black knee length skirt and shoes that looked comfortable enough for someone on her feet all day. Natural grey had been allowed to show through brown shoulder length hair, enhancing her maturity, something which a bottle of dye would have certainly ruined, thought Maddie.

'Talk of the devil,' he said.

'What have I done now?' The woman's soft brown eyes regarded them quizzically, her attention settling on the young woman standing before her.

Her husband spoke. 'The young lady here was wondering about one of the pictures over there. I told her you're the expert.'

'Oh yes?' she smiled warmly, appraising the younger woman. It wasn't normally the youngsters that expressed an interest in any of the old photographs and she was pleasantly surprised. 'Which one would that be then?

Maddie went over to the photo. 'It's this one here.'

The woman placed the tray of glasses on the bar before joining her. Without further discourse, she looked thoughtfully at the picture for a second or two. 'Oh yes – I remember this one alright. That's the Pengelly family. They had a small holding about four miles from here across the moor. Most were farmers or miners back then, until the copper mines closed around the end of the eighteen hundred's...' She paused, looking at Maddie. 'Can I ask – what interests you about this particular picture?'

Maddie raised her eyebrows at the direct question. 'Oh – nothing especially. Just curious, that's all – do you know anything about the little girl?'

The woman looked back at the photo. 'That was their daughter, Rose. Pretty little thing, isn't she?'

'Rose,' Maddie breathed, as if the very mention of her name might reveal something to her. 'Do you know how old she was when the photo was taken?'

The woman shook her head. 'Afraid not – no. Best guess would be around nine or ten I'd say. The photo was taken not long before the tragedy struck the family.'

'Tragedy?'

'I'm afraid so. It's a sad tale to say the least – according to what the locals have told me anyhow. Whether there's any truth to it or not – well I've only got their word for it.'

Maddie was intrigued. 'What happened?'

The woman gathered her thoughts before recounting the story. 'Rose was their only daughter and they doted on her. There are been complications during Rose's birth which meant her mother couldn't have any more children. Anyway – she'd been out playing around the farm like she usually did but one day a heavy mist had descended and she never returned. Her father rode out on horseback looking for any sign of her on the moor whilst his distraught wife waited at home in the hope she might turn up. A few hours later her husband returned, the lifeless body of their daughter slung over the saddle in front of him. Inconsolable, his wife died not long after from a broken heart.'

Maddie listened in silence.

The woman slowly shook her head. 'Poor thing must have strayed too far from the farm, got lost in the fog and wandered off into a bog somewhere.'

'That's terrible,' Maddie finally said.

'It is indeed. Of course, there's more to the story,' she carried on. 'For some of the locals claim the little girl haunts the moor to this very day...'

'Oh! really?' Maddie felt the hairs prick up on her neck.

'Yes. But she only appears at certain times; to those unlucky enough to find themselves lost on the moor and helps guide them back to safety – so the story goes anyway. Though, to be honest, I've never heard first hand from anyone who was lost on the moor and encountered Rose's spirit. It wouldn't surprise me if that part of the story had been embellished over the years to serve the local tourism.'

Maddie appeared dreamy. 'It almost sounds like the poor thing is atoning for her own unfortunate demise and feels compelled now to help the living.'

'Yes, that would be a good way of describing it,' the woman nodded. 'It's a fanciful tale, that's for sure. But the moor does have a reputation for being very unforgiving when the weather changes and many an unsuspecting traveller has been caught out trying to cross it over the years. Plenty of marshland and bogs out there too. It's not uncommon even now for a farmer to have to drag one of his sheep or cows out of the bog with a tractor, you know.'

For a moment, Maddie couldn't speak, her mind reeling from the revelation. 'I didn't know that. I just thought areas like that would have been fenced off to the public. For safety reasons, I mean.'

The woman just shook her head dolefully.

Maddie felt that the woman had little else to reveal now and she wanted nothing more than to sit down for a while in quiet reflection. Taking her eyes from the photo she turned to the woman. 'You've been very helpful. Thanks for the information.'

The woman smiled faintly. 'Your welcome. If there's anything else I can help you with don't be afraid to ask?' She prided herself on her local knowledge, but she'd detected an edginess in the young woman's voice that told her the discourse was now over.

Maddie smiled back. 'Thanks, but I've already taken up more than enough of your time.'

The woman joined her husband at the bar, leaving Maddie alone to ponder the picture and the strange story surrounding it. Was the Rose in the photo the same little girl she'd encountered on the moor? They shared an uncanny resemblance, yes. But it couldn't be – could it? It was impossible. Yet part of her wanted it to be true.

She wandered back to her seat, her mind still struggling to make sense of it all and Jodie looked up nonchalantly from her phone. 'I was about to send out a search party. Thought you'd got lost?'

Maddie sat, and moments later a thought occurred to her. 'Have you got your map handy? There's something I want to check.'

'It's right here,' Jodie said, pulling it from her back pocket. 'What are you looking for?'

'The derelict house we stayed in?'

'What about it?'

'Can you find it on the map. Roughly where it was I mean?'

Jodie looked thoughtful. 'I should be able to,

but it won't be exact of course.'

They cleared some space on the table and Jodie unfolded the map. Maddie got into position behind her so she could see over her shoulder.

'Here's Jamaica Inn.' Jodie tapped it with her finger. 'And here's the trail that brought us here. So...four miles back would be roughly... let's see...around about here.'

Maddie scrutinised the area where Jodie's finger rested. She was unfamiliar with maps and the funny looking symbols used to denote the various ground features, but if she could just find what she was looking for it might confirm her suspicions.

'So, what is it you're not telling me – huh?' Jodie asked, looking puzzled.

'So, that's the path that forks in two, isn't it?' Maddie inquired, ignoring the direct question.

Jodie checked for a moment. 'Yes – that would be right.'

'And this little blue area here? Maddie circled it with her finger. 'What's does this mean?'

Jodie recognised the map symbol, and looked up at Maddie. 'Blue means water of some kind, either a river, a stream or a lake perhaps. Now, in this case,' she explained, looking back down and tapping the symbol with her finger. 'These markings inside the blue area that look like little reeds or tufts of grass would indicate its marshland or a bog. It's a warning symbol. You wouldn't want to go wandering in there by mistake, would you?'

Maddie went quiet, came around to her side of the table and sat down again. There was no denying it now, no matter how bizarre or unbelievable it seemed. Whichever way she tried analysing it the fact remained that the little girl had distracted her from taking that path, a route that would have taken her through the bogs and marshes of the wetlands and in that heavy mist...? Maddie shuddered at the thought.

Jodie was folding up the map. 'So, going to tell me what this is all about Maddie? You've been acting very funny since you came back from the loo. And another thing? What was that woman talking to you about over there? I saw the pair of you looking at that picture.'

A knowing smile touched Maddie's lips as she looked across the table at her friend. 'Have I,' she said softly. 'Oh – it's nothing to worry about – honestly Jodie. I don't know about you though – but I could murder another coffee right now.'

EPILOGUE

Two weeks had passed since her hike around the moor and Maddie was sitting at the kitchen table looking at the photos she'd taken on her phone. The Beast of Bodmin Moor had eluded her, the sweat and grime had been washed away long ago, the itchiness in her scalp just a distant memory now along with the pesky insect that had sucked on her blood. None of it mattered now.

'Maddie?' her mum hollered.

'What's up?'

'You might want to see this. Quick!'

She slid off the seat and wandered nonchalantly into the room next door.

Mum was sat on the couch watching the West Country News. 'This might interest you.'

'What is it?' She sat down next to her and went quiet as she listened to the news report, wondering what possible relevance it might have to her.

They were library pictures of Bodmin Moor and something about a man's body that had been discovered by a farmer after his dog started barking towards a notorious area of marshland. A reporter was interviewing some shocked locals who had known the deceased. They couldn't understand why he had been out there in the first place as his van had been discovered outside his cottage and there was no indication he had been rabbiting or shooting. The man had worked around the moor for years and knew the dangers that it posed. It was all a bit of a mystery, to say the least. Some people said he was a bit of a loner and liked to keep himself to himself. A bit of an odd ball and never seen without that red base-ball cap he always wore. Yet others, who had known him well, said there was a darker side to the man. One minute he was nice as pie and the next he could fly into an unprovoked rage. It was almost as if he had some sort of split personality.

The farmer had already given his account to the local newspaper reporter who'd wasted no time in seeking him out as soon as the story had broken. Visibly shaken from his ordeal, the farmer recounted the gruesome discovery that would haunt him for the rest of his days. The image of a man in a bog, his head the only thing visible from the chin up while his upright torso lay submerged beneath a quagmire of stagnant water thick with aquatic plant life. The dead man's eyes were frozen wide open, his deathly white face contorted into a mask of terror, as if the poor fellow had been aware of his impending demise and had died from fright long before hunger, thirst or hypothermia had set in. How long he'd been there was anyone's guess.

It was too early to say yet, but the police didn't suspect foul play because there'd been no obvious marks found on the body but they guessed the unfortunate man had simply got lost in the mist and wandered into the bog. The thirty-five-year-old was known locally as Ben Smith. A post mortem was scheduled for next Monday and would reveal more.

'Lucky that wasn't you pair,' mum remarked.

Maddie couldn't tear her eyes away from the television. 'God! I wonder if Jodie's seen this?'

18945751R00150

Printed in Poland
by Amazon Fulfillment
Poland Sp. z o.o., Wrocław